# IT HAD TO BE YOU

Paula arrives in Kinbrae, hoping to make a success of the café she's taken over. There are a few hiccups along the way, but with the help of the former owner's son, Jack, she begins to settle in nicely. Widower Jack has a teenaged daughter and runs his own business. He's not looking for a love interest — but he finds he suddenly can't stop thinking about Paula. And when Paula's ex-fiancé turns up and asks her to go back to London with him, Jack has to make a decision . . .

SUZANNE ROSS JONES

# IT HAD TO BE YOU

*Complete and Unabridged*

**LINFORD**
*Leicester*

First published in Great Britain in 2013

First Linford Edition
published 2015

A catalogue record for this book is available
from the British Library.

ISBN 978–1–4448–2261–8

Published by
F. A. Thorpe (Publishing)
Anstey, Leicestershire

Set by Words & Graphics Ltd.
Anstey, Leicestershire
Printed and bound in Great Britain by
T. J. International Ltd., Padstow, Cornwall

This book is printed on acid-free paper

# A New Start

Paula Dixon grabbed her pencil and notebook from the counter and approached the only occupied table in her newly acquired café. This was it: her very first customer. She took a deep breath and then smiled, desperate to make a good impression.

The woman, probably a few years older than Paula's own mother, sat with arms crossed, looking around her with lips pursed and a frown on her face.

'Good morning.' Paula's smile remained as bright as the morning sunshine and she eagerly anticipated that the customer would reciprocate.

She was disappointed.

'Thursday's an odd day to open a café.'

Paula blinked. But, professional that she was, she managed to keep her smile firmly pinned in place.

'Er, I suppose it is.' Although, she wasn't sure any other day would have been better. 'I wanted to start trading as soon as I was ready; there didn't seem much point in hanging on.'

'You've painted the walls.'

It didn't sound like a compliment. Paula's smile dimmed a tad. 'Yes, I did. Do you the colour? I thought yellow would be a nice and bright.'

'And the chairs.' The woman shifted around on her chair. 'You've brought in new chairs. And tables.'

Paula nodded. In truth, she'd been left with little choice. The café was charming — of course it was; she wouldn't have bought the place other-wise — but the furniture had been a health and safety hazard. The chairs had been so rickety it was a wonder they hadn't collapsed under the weight of even the lightest customer.

Paula guessed, however, that it wouldn't do to say anything that might be mistaken for criticism of the previous owner. Not only had the McGregors run this café for generations, but Heather McGregor was an absolute sweetheart. She'd even told Paula to call if she needed any help or had any questions.

'Cake?' the woman demanded.

'Yes.' Paula was relieved to be able to reassure her on that point, at least. 'Yes, we have cake.' She waved towards the counter to where an impressive display sat behind protective glass. 'Would you like to come over and choose what kind you'd like?'

'Not really. It's too early for cake. It's not even nine o'clock yet. I want to know if you made those cakes yourself.'

Paula blushed a guilty pink. She'd love to be able to say she had, but the display was the result of a visit to the specialist cake shop in the nearest large town. Paula didn't bake — which had been one of her mother's objections to her buying into business.

'They were made by a very talented baker — I'm sure you'll have no complaint.'

'Hmm. So you didn't make them.

Heather McGregor always made her own cakes. What's the point in people coming in here to eat cake that wasn't made on the premises?' The question hung in the air and Paula cringed.

Looked like her mother had been right about the baking after all. She was going to have to learn how to make cakes.

'What's this?' The customer prodded at the hard case that sat on the table.

Paula paused with her pencil midway to her notebook and frowned. 'Er . . . it's a laptop.'

The woman cast a withering glance. 'I know it's a laptop. I'm not an idiot. What's it doing here on this table?'

Paula smiled again and prepared to deliver the sales speech she'd rehearsed to entice customers through the door. This idea was a winner — she was sure even this fussy customer wouldn't be able to argue with that. 'We now offer free internet access here at McGregor's.' She smiled.

'Whatever for?'

That threw her for a moment. She hadn't expected such a question. 'We feel it will enhance our customers' visits here,' she said at last.

The woman snorted. 'Oh, no. That will never take on.'

Paula's smile was a little less bright as she continued with the pitch. 'We've done our market research. It brings valuable custom to other cafés.'

The woman's eyes narrowed. 'We?' she queried. 'I thought you'd taken this place over on your own.'

Paula sighed. She suddenly wished she'd never started this conversation. Her first mistake had probably been to say 'good morning', she realised. It had given the woman an excuse to talk back.

'Yes, it's just me.'

'Then where's this 'we' you're talking about coming from?'

This time, Paula's smile was decidedly forced. She wondered if all the customers in Kinbrae were going to be this awkward.

No, she refused to think like that. She was going to be positive. Especially as Heather McGregor had told her the locals were lovely.

'I was referring to the business.' It was obvious the woman wasn't impressed. Paula sighed. 'The 'we' was supposed to be professional and business-like.'

The woman shook her head. 'It was neither of those things.'

At that point, Paula very nearly asked why the woman had bothered to come in if all she was going to do was to find fault. But she remembered in time that she shouldn't really be arguing with customers.

'What can I get for you this morning?' she asked instead, in an attempt to divert any more questions.

'Do you know, I don't think I'll bother, after all. This place isn't what it was when Heather McGregor was running things.' There was a scraping of wooden chair legs against the tiled floor.

'Why don't you stay and have a cup of tea?' Paula suggested, still keen to make a good impression. 'On the house. As a reward for being my first customer.'

The woman threaded her arms into her coat and picked up her handbag. It seemed tea wasn't going to do the trick.

'I'll throw in a pastry.' Paula smiled again. But the woman wasn't having any of it.

'Three generations of McGregor women have run this place,' she said. 'And, if you count Heather's sons, four generations have stood behind that counter. It just isn't the same now you're here.'

Paula sighed as she watched the woman retreat towards the door.

*Welcome to Kinbrae, Paula*, she thought to herself. She suspected fitting in was going to be tougher than she'd imagined.

Foolish, her mother had said, to use her savings on a venture that was barely breaking even. Especially when that business was hundreds of miles away from her friends and family and everything familiar. And especially when she had no experience of working in catering or dealing directly with customers.

She'd needed to do something, though, and she'd had a good feeling about this place as soon as she'd arrived to look around. She was positive she could make things work here, and one difficult local resident hadn't changed her mind about that.

In her haste to leave the café, Paula's non-customer cannoned into a man who was just stepping through the door. A tall, red-haired man. Paula's heart lifted. She hoped he might stay long enough to order something.

'Hello, Joyce.' He grinned and the woman, who it seemed was called Joyce, smiled back. Admittedly it was a bit of a frosty smile, but those lips were definitely turning upwards. Good to know she was able — Paula had begun to doubt it.

'How are you this morning?' He held the door open for Joyce to make her exit.

'I'm fine, thank you, Jack. Didn't expect to see you here today.' She cast a frosty glance in Paula's direction. 'Not now things have changed so much around here. How's your mother?'

'She's fine, thank you. I'll let her know you were asking after her.'

Joyce nodded, pulled her handbag closer to her body and, with head down, left the premises at top speed.

He turned his attention to Paula. 'I'm guessing Joyce was here to have a look about the place.'

Paula winced. She couldn't help it. The man's blue eyes crinkled at the corners as he laughed. 'Don't take any notice. She's always found fault with the place, so consider yourself accepted if she's decided you're worth her time.'

Paula smiled. Good to know the grumpy Joyce hadn't singled her out. 'That's a positive way to look at it.'

'The only way to look at it, if you want to survive in Kinbrae. The locals mean well, but they can be outspoken at times.' He glanced around the café.

'You've done a lot with the place in a week.'

She smiled. 'I work fast when I put my mind to it. I wanted to open as quickly as possible and I wanted my own stamp on the place.'

'But you've kept the name?'

'McGregor's came with a lot of goodwill. Although Joyce made it clear it wouldn't be the same without a real McGregor behind the counter.' She sighed.

Her customer smiled. 'You're Paula, aren't you?'

Paula's eyes narrowed. 'How do you know that?'

'Local grapevine.'

She nodded. That made sense. She held out her hand to make the meeting formal and he folded his own, larger one around it.

'And I heard Joyce calling you Jack?'

'See, you're learning the Kinbrae ways of discovering information already. Watch, listen and absorb. Nothing is secret here for long.'

His handshake was firm and strong

10

and he smiled, showing a row of even, white teeth.

She nodded. 'I suppose it's like that in all small towns.' She waved an arm about the room. 'You can sit anywhere you like. As you can see, I'm not busy.'

'I'd really love to stay, but I'm on my way to work. I only popped in this morning to see how you were doing.'

'Oh.' The emotional punch of another disappointment rendered her almost speechless — a second potential customer would be leaving without ordering anything.

He seemed to pick up on her mood and offered an apologetic smile. 'But as I'm here,' he added, 'I didn't stop for breakfast this morning, so a black coffee to take away would be just the thing.'

Paula resisted the urge to happy-dance on the spot. This man — this lovely Jack, whoever he was — had made her morning by ordering a coffee.

She grinned. 'On the house,' she offered as she put the lid on the polystyrene cup and handed him his hot drink. 'And have some proper breakfast, too,' she said, picking up her tongs and putting the largest blueberry muffin from her display into a paper bag.

His fingers were warm as they brushed hers as he took the muffin and he smiled. 'That's no way to run a business. You'll never make a profit if you don't charge your customers.'

'This is a one-off,' she laughed. 'A special offer for my very first order ever. You can pay for the next one.'

'OK, deal. I might be in tomorrow. Nothing like home baking for breakfast.'

'Er . . . ' Paula could feel her face getting warmer. 'I suppose I should confess. I've bought the cakes in from the bakery in town.'

He shook his head. 'That's a very expensive way to do it.'

'I know. I'm hoping to start making my own cakes and pastries once I'm settled.' She smiled, hoping that he wouldn't notice the tremor in her hand as she contemplated that particular task.

# The Scone Man

The evidence of something burning reached Jack's nose as soon as he opened the door to McGregor's the next day. He was in for another takeaway coffee and perhaps a muffin, and he was pleased to see the place marginally busier than it had been yesterday: a couple he didn't know were occupying a table.

But the smell did worry him. And Paula didn't seem to have noticed either it or him. He glanced above the door — the bell was missing. She'd probably taken it down when she'd been decorating. If it had been there, at least she would have noticed him.

As things stood, she remained oblivious — deep in conversation with the young couple, stopping only to laugh as she took their order. The three were so animated and noisy that perhaps she wouldn't have noticed he'd arrived even with the bell.

He stood for a moment watching her laugh. And the sound made him want to laugh along with her. She tucked a dark strand of hair that had come loose from her ponytail back behind her ear. It didn't look as though she was planning to deal with whatever was burning anytime soon.

'Paula,' he spoke when he knew it wouldn't wait a moment longer.

She looked up and her face broke into a smile — a very lovely smile, he couldn't help noticing. 'Hello, Jack. I'll be with you in a minute.'

'I think there might be a bit of an emergency in the kitchen,' he told her.

He didn't wait for her to react, but headed through to the back and made straight for the oven. As soon as he opened the door, smoke billowed out. Simultaneously, Jack coughed and the fire alarm screamed into action.

Paula burst in after him and he saw a look of horror on her face. 'Oh, no!' she called over the incessant bleeping of the alarm. 'I'd forgotten I had something in the oven. It was just so nice to have customers who wanted to order breakfast and were happy to chat.'

Jack grabbed oven gloves from the work surface, then took hold of the offending baking tray with the charred remains of what looked as though they might once have been scones.

'Can you open the back door, please, and I'll get rid of this,' he said.

It was good to be away from the smoke-filled kitchen. Jack set the baking tray down on the ground of the café's tiny back yard, then paused a moment to breathe clear air into his lungs.

Paula came to the door, wafting the smoke outside with a tea towel. 'I can't believe I did that. I just completely forgot.' Her voice was a bit wobbly and her big brown eyes were over-bright. He hoped she wasn't going to start crying. The only female tears Jack could deal with were those of his daughter. And he was never happy about those, either.

'Easily done.' His voice was calm as he tried to reassure her. 'You got distracted, forget the time . . . '

'You don't understand.' She was visibly upset now, her nose growing red and her eyes looking very wet.

Oh, yes, Jack realised with a sinking heart. Tears were most definitely on the agenda. And he couldn't help but think that they were out of proportion with the situation. After all, what had actually happened here? She'd lost a few scones and perhaps the baking tray.

'No.' He raked his hand through his hair. 'No, I don't understand.'

'Everyone was waiting for me to fail at this.' She sniffed. 'My mother, my ex-colleagues . . . everyone. They all told me this was a mistake. And now I've proved them right.'

He didn't like that she was crying. He thought about how he dealt with Jessica when there were tears and decided to take the same tack. Uncertainly at first, he put his arms around her, and when

16

she didn't object he drew her closer for a hug.

'You haven't failed. This is only your second day open. You've got a long way to go before you've failed at anything.'

'That's not true.' She sniffed against his shirt. 'I burnt the scones. The easiest thing in the world to make, my mother told me. And I couldn't even manage that.'

He frowned. 'I thought you were going to buy everything in for the time being. Why did you decide to bake when you're still busy getting settled in?'

She took a breath. 'I was reacting to customer feedback. You and Joyce were both shocked that I was getting everything from the baker's.'

So this was partly his fault. That didn't make him feel any better. He patted her on the back in what he hoped was a comforting gesture. 'Burnt scones aren't a sign of failure.'

'No?' She lifted her head and bright brown eyes regarded him with a disbelieving gleam. 'Maybe not. But I haven't sold a single thing. After you left yesterday nobody came in. Nobody at all. I knew business was going to be slow; Heather McGregor warned me it would be quiet, especially at this time of year. But not one single person bought anything all day.'

'You've got two customers in at the moment,' he reminded her.

'Oh.' A fleeting expression of panic crossed her face and she ducked out of his arms and disappeared through the kitchen and into the café.

She was back only moments later. 'They've gone.'

'Oh.' He didn't know what else to say. Her disappointment was tangible and he feared there would be more tears. So he did what he always did when he didn't know what words to say: he took action and he stepped back towards the kitchen with Paula following close behind.

'What are you doing?' she asked as he simultaneously shrugged off his jacket and began to dial on his mobile.

'Showing you how to make scones.' He grinned and then spoke into his phone. 'Claire, hi. It's Jack. I've been held up. Can you clear my diary for this morning, please? . . . Great. I'll be in as soon as I can.'

'No,' Paula objected as he slipped the phone back into his pocket. 'I couldn't possibly let you do that.' She was genuinely horrified, and her expression made him want to laugh.

'And I can't possibly leave you when you're upset and in need of fresh scones.'

'But your work . . . '

He shook his head. 'Claire's a good assistant. She'll take care of everything until I get back.'

'She's going to have to take care of everything at your work because you're going to make scones for my café?' There was an incredulous quality to her voice — as though she didn't quite believe what she was saying. 'That's just . . . Well, it's not that I don't appreciate the offer, but that's plain daft.' She sniffed loudly.

19

The strange thing was, women who were prone to irrational tears normally made Jack very uncomfortable. Not that he made a habit of bumping into women who were upset, but he knew that had any other woman of his acquaintance cried over burnt scones, he'd have excused himself just as soon as he was sure she was OK.

But for some reason he was still worried about Paula. Her tears had dried, but she was still to recover her earlier bounce. And that made him suspect she was still upset. He didn't want her to be upset and all on her own. Leaving her now wouldn't be the neighbourly thing to do — especially as she was new in town and he knew she was yet to make friends.

And, even though he should have been at work, he smiled because he'd much rather be exactly where he was. For the moment.

'I disagree,' he told her calmly. 'I think it's very sensible. You need scones and I know how to make them.' He slung his jacket over the back of a chair and rolled up his sleeves before scrubbing his hands at the sink. 'Your mother's right — they are easy. But, as with everything else in life, you have to know what you're doing.'

★   ★   ★

That was the whole point. Paula didn't have a clue what she was doing. And not only with the scones. She'd been so sure that a complete change of direction — personal and professional — had been the right thing for her. But things weren't working out the way she'd hoped.

She sighed as she watched Jack measure out flour with a spoon. He didn't even use the scales. She'd been meticulous and weighed everything — followed the recipe down to the last detail. Except she'd forgotten all about the scones once she'd put them in the oven.

Maybe she'd been hasty leaving her

21

old job. OK, there had been *that* incident — the one that still had the ability to turn her blood cold if she thought about it too much. But at least she'd known what she was doing with computers. Most of the time, in any case. They were logical, and cause and effect were easily identified. And she hadn't allowed a single one to catch fire.

Scones were a different matter — at least as far as she was concerned. Jack was making swift work of it as he popped a tray into the oven.

'You made that look incredibly easy,' she told him. 'Don't tell me you can make cakes and pastries, too.'

He looked slightly embarrassed. 'Actually, I can.'

'Oh, that's so not fair.'

His cheek dimpled as he smiled and she couldn't help noticing how good-looking he was. And she couldn't help smiling back at him.

'Actually,' he continued, 'I spent a lot of time here at the café as I was growing up — helping out.'

'You worked here?'

He nodded. 'Every weekend and holiday from the age of fourteen until I left school and went to university at eighteen. I even lived in the flat upstairs that last summer.'

'You did?' She didn't know quite how she felt, knowing Jack had once lived in the tiny flat she now occupied.

He nodded. 'I was trying to assert my independence. And it was handy and meant I could be in here nice and early to get a head start on the baking.'

She laughed. 'No wonder you know what you're doing in this kitchen. Even I know Heather McGregor's cakes are legendary. If you worked for the woman for four years . . . '

He grinned.

'Maybe I should see if she's free to give me some lessons.' Paula was only making conversation. Despite the other woman's offer of help, Paula didn't imagine for a moment Heather would be interested in coming back to the café she'd sold. Not even on a temporary basis.

But a glint appeared in Jack's blue eyes and he rubbed his chin thoughtfully. 'That might be an idea. You could ask her if she'd give you a hand. Just until you find your feet.'

'Oh, I don't know . . . ' she blustered, her face warming as she realised he'd taken her seriously. 'I mean it would hardly be fair. If she wanted to be here she wouldn't have sold up.'

'Well I can't work out why she sold the place, so you might be surprised,' he told her. 'Besides, she's also quite bossy and she might enjoy the experience of telling you what to do.'

Paula laughed — she couldn't imagine the charming woman she'd met doing anything of the sort.

'I think they're ready,' he said, still grinning.

She watched and was quietly impressed as he brought out a tray of perfect golden scones and presented them with a flourish.

'Well, if you're ever looking for a job . . . '

His laughter started as a low rumble and then took over his features as his blue eyes crinkled at the corners. 'Believe me, I've paid my dues in this place, but I don't think I'll be back in the kitchen on a permanent basis.'

'And I suppose you have a more interesting job now?'

'I think so. I work at JM Structural Engineers in town.'

Paula could see why he'd been tempted away from the café. 'I don't suppose I can match the kind of salary package and opportunity for career progression they can offer.' She sighed loudly and Jack laughed as he grabbed his jacket.

'I'm not in it so much for the money — although that's useful. It's more because it's something I enjoy.'

'I can understand that.' That was how Paula had once felt about IT.

'Speaking of my career, I'd better get back to it. But I just have time to reattach the bell above your door before I go.'

'Well, thank you, Mr . . . '

'I think you know me well enough that you can call me Jack,' he told her. 'But it's McGregor — Jack McGregor.'

Realisation dawned. 'So that's why you worked here. Heather must be your — '

He nodded. 'She's my mum,' he confirmed.

# A Visit from Heather McGregor

Jack picked up the phone and dialled as soon as he got to the office. Heather answered almost immediately. 'Hi, Ma. It's me, Jack. How are things?'

'Quiet, you know. I'm still not used to not having the café to go to. And I miss the customers.'

There was something quite wrong with this picture. He knew how much his mother had loved the café. She'd started working behind the counter while she was still a schoolgirl. Jack's Granny McGregor had taken over the running of the place from his great-grandmother by then. And it had caused a storm of gossip when Heather had married the boss's son not long after leaving school.

And now she'd admitted missing the place.

'I still don't understand why you got rid of the café.' It was well documented that Heather had been utterly devoted to McGregor's. Apart from the odd holiday and three lots of maternity leave, she'd been in to open up bright and early every single morning.

'Well, you know. I worked there for years and it was time for a change. And the right person came along to take over.'

The answer was vague and unsubstantial. Jack suspected his mother was evading the issue and he made a mental note to get to grips with the situation and demand an answer. But that was best done in person. Face to face, it would be easier to ferret out the truth.

'She's struggling, you know.'

'Who?'

'The right person. Nobody's going near the place.'

He heard his mother's heavy intake of breath. 'I was worried something like that might happen. But this is only her second day open. People will come round. They just need time to adjust.'

'Why don't you pop in and offer support? If they see you in there they might think it's acceptable to go in, too.'

'Are things really that bad? How do you know?'

'I popped by yesterday to wish her luck. Joyce Imrie was in giving her a hard time.'

'Well I hope you told her to take no notice.'

'I did.' He laughed at his mother's indignant tone. 'And I told her when I went in this morning that she shouldn't worry about the other locals — that they would come round eventually.'

There was a telling silence down the line. He could almost hear his mother's mind working and he kind of wished he hadn't said anything about his two visits to Paula Dixon. But if he hadn't, she would doubtless have heard all about them from someone else — and then she would be even more suspicious.

'So, you've been to see her two days running?'

'We can't let her flounder. It's our name above her door.'

'If you're not careful,' she said, and he could hear the smile in her voice, 'your visits could become a habit.'

And he smiled too, even though he knew that was true. 'I went in to see how she was. And for coffee to take to work.'

'So you don't have a coffee machine in your office these days?'

He chuckled softly. But he didn't admit to his mother that she was right — that it wasn't the coffee that was the attraction.

Or that it would be very easy to drop in on Paula every day.

Far too easy.

★　★　★

Paula was wiping tables — even though nobody had been near the place to dirty them since Jack had left a couple of hours earlier. But it was as well to keep the place looking nice, just in case.

It was nearly lunchtime now. Maybe someone would come in for a sandwich and a cup of tea.

She heard the door open and turned around, her heart filled with hope. But although her visitor wasn't a customer, her smile held genuine warmth when she saw who was there. She'd liked Heather McGregor very much the few times she'd met her and she was pleased to see her now.

Heather smiled back. 'I stayed away as long as I could,' she said. 'But I'm dying to see what you've done with the place.'

Paula showed the former owner around — not that there was much to see, really. Apart from the main tea room, there was a smaller room that Heather had used for storage, but that Paula had painted and furnished with a few tables.

'I thought once I get a customer base established, I could offer birthday teas or a place for private meetings.'

Heather nodded. 'Good idea. I wish

I'd thought of it when I was running the place. Denny and the boys were always telling me it was a waste of good space to use this as a storeroom. Especially with the big larder cupboard in the kitchen.'

Paula smiled. 'Can I offer you a coffee?' she asked.

'That would be lovely, thank you.' Heather walked back into the tea room proper and sat at a window seat, looking out on the small patio area outside. 'What about the tables for outside? Did you get rid of them when you cleared the storeroom?'

'As if.' Paula laughed. 'They were partly what attracted me to the café. The first time I saw the place, the tables were outside and everyone was sitting in the sun. It reminded me of holidays in France and Italy.' She brought a tray with two coffees and some scones and jam. 'The outdoor furniture is in the shed, ready for the next warm, sunny day.'

Heather stirred a spoonful of soft

brown sugar into her coffee and poured in cream. 'It's really odd being on this side of things.'

'I can imagine it is. It's pretty odd for me, too.' Paula's sigh was heavy.

Heather nodded sympathetically. 'It's a long time since I first started working in this café, but I do remember what it was like. You will get used to it.' She reached for a scone.

'Your son made these,' Paula said, also helping herself from the plate she'd brought over.

'Jack?'

Paula nodded, remembering that Heather had three sons — although Jack was the only one she'd met so far.

'He came in this morning and found me in a bit of a muddle with the baking.'

Heather's glance was thoughtful and Paula worried she might have spoken out of turn. Was Heather the type of mother to read too much into a statement like that?

'So you two have been getting along?'

It seemed she was exactly that type of mother. Paula shrugged. 'We barely know each other. He's been in for coffee twice — and helped out with the scones that second time.'

'He's been on his own a long time.' Heather took a sip of her coffee. 'He was widowed barely into the second year of his marriage.'

It hadn't even occurred to Paula that Jack might have been married — he hadn't given off that vibe. This news was a bit of a shock. And it wasn't pleasant to hear that a young woman had lost her life.

'Oh, I'm so sorry. That must have been tough on all of you.'

'It wasn't the easiest time. But Jack's worked hard building his business and raising his daughter, Jessica. He's a good dad.'

So, he was a family man. Yes, she could see that. Paula thought back to how kind he had been when faced with her tears this morning.

'I imagine he is.'

Heather split her scone in two and added a spoonful of jam before biting into it. 'Good to know the lad hasn't lost his touch. When he was at school he used to help out here.'

'I know; he said.'

Heather raised an eyebrow.

'He was explaining how he learned to make scones.'

Heather smiled. 'My boys all helped out at the café when they were teenagers. I think probably working with their dad on the lorries would have been better for their street cred, but I paid a higher hourly rate.'

Paula laughed. 'It must have been a difficult choice for them.' She took a sip of her coffee. 'Actually . . . ' She looked around. 'I think I would have loved a place like this to hang around in when I was young. Even now, even if I didn't own the place, I think I'd love to pop in for a sit-down and cake — and to meet friends.'

Heather tapped her fingers on the table for a moment, her far-away expression suggesting she was deep in thought. Then her frown cleared. 'You know, Paula, I think I might have an idea for how you could drum up some trade.'

Paula sat back in her chair. 'I'm listening.'

'Well, what you were saying about popping in to meet friends . . . We have a few young families in Kinbrae — where mum, and sometimes the odd dad, stays at home with a young baby. And I know some of them don't always get out as much as they'd like.'

Paula frowned. 'You think I should cater to babies?'

Heather laughed. 'No, not the babies, exactly. Their parents. To be honest, I had thought of trying something similar myself. I didn't really have the space to do the idea justice, but you have that additional room now. You could do a special offer one or two mornings a week: tea or coffee and a cake for a small discount if the purchaser brings a baby. And you already have the facilities to heat up baby food.'

'Hmmm.' Paula thought about this suggestion. 'That's a good idea. I like it.'

'Look, the health visitor is a friend of mine. Why don't I have a word with her, and she can mention it to her mums. And you could put a notice in the window.' Heather glanced out to the street and smiled as a couple stopped to wave at her. 'And, in the meantime, I'll sit here a little longer so I'm seen, and maybe that will bring one or two of my old customers through the door.'

'I can't believe you're helping me like this.'

'That's still my name above the door, even if the café no longer belongs to a McGregor,' she explained softly. 'And I can't stand by and watch as the locals try to make up their minds whether they're going to accept you. They need a nudge. And I'm happy to provide it.'

'In that case — ' Paula got to her feet as she spoke. ' — the least I can do is top up your coffee.'

*  *  *

If seeing Heather McGregor sitting in the window drinking coffee and eating scones hadn't quite brought a full miracle to pass, it had performed a small trick. Slowly, as the afternoon progressed, a trickle of customers came through her door. And they bought teas and coffees, and the odd one even bought a cake.

Admittedly, they didn't buy many coffees or much cake, but it was enough so that after she'd closed and carried out the necessary cleaning, she had to cash up because there was some actual, real money in the till.

'Not bad, Paula,' she told herself as she slipped the money into her handbag ready to pay into the bank tomorrow. 'Not bad at all.' Although she knew there was still a long way to go.

One of the advantages to not selling all the stock, though, was the leftovers. She made up one of the cardboard take-away cake boxes and she helped herself to a couple of cakes that would be past their best by tomorrow. She glanced at Jack's scones. She'd eaten one when Heather was in earlier — and it had been good. Almost as an afterthought, she popped one of the scones into the box, too. If the cakes were to be her supper, she could have the scone for her breakfast.

After she climbed the stairs to the flat, she switched on the computer and made a start on the posters Heather had suggested for the parent and baby coffee mornings. Heather had been so convinced it would be a good idea that Paula had to give it a go. She made a half dozen — one for her own café, and she planned to ask the other businesses in Kinbrae if they might consider displaying one in their windows, too. Again, that had been Heather's idea — quite apart from the increased exposure for the café, it would give Paula a chance to meet some of her new neighbours.

As the last one printed off and she gave it a quick proof-read, the phone rang. Paula looked at it in mild surprise. Apart from her mother, nobody had called her since she had moved in here. That was the sort of thing that happened when your social life had been centred around your job — and you left that job under something of a cloud. Most people you'd thought were your friends just didn't want to know.

And the one person she had counted on since childhood — her very best friend in the world, the one who had stood by her throughout her recent turmoil — was on her honeymoon. There was no way it would be Ellie — she wouldn't be calling, not from Hawaii.

She also knew it wouldn't be her mother — Nancy Dixon had a busy life and her phone calls to her daughter were strictly rationed to one a week. And, as this wasn't Sunday, it couldn't be her.

So, who could it be?

With a sigh, she realised there was only one way to find out. She picked up the receiver. 'Paula Dixon speaking.'

'Paula, hi. I hope I'm not disturbing you?'

'Hi Jack.' She smiled — she couldn't help it. 'Of course you aren't. How can I help you?'

'I passed by earlier — saw you had a few customers in.'

'A few, yes. All thanks to your mother. She popped in and made sure she was seen drinking her coffee.'

He chuckled softly. 'I'm glad she helped.'

'Your scones went down well,' she told him with a smile. 'Are you sure I can't tempt you to take on a part-time job here as my baker?'

'This is where I should probably admit that even though I worked in the café for years, scones are the only things I truly mastered.'

'I thought you said you could make cakes and pastries.'

'Well, I can,' he added with a laugh. 'And they were mostly passable. But definitely not up to my mother's standard.'

She laughed, pleased to know he wasn't perfect at everything after all. 'Scones are still more than I can make,' she reminded him.

'Speaking of cakes — which we were in a roundabout way — I know the café's closed, but I wonder if there's any way I could buy some of those cakes you have in your display cabinet.'

'What? Now?'

'Please — if that's possible. Jessica, my daughter, has friends round for a movie night — there's talk of taking pizzas out of the freezer. And I'm in the doghouse because I forgot to buy puddings.'

'Oh dear, I see why you need emergency cake.'

'So? Can I pop over?'

'I'll meet you in the café in five minutes.'

'Or . . . '

She frowned down the line. 'Or, what?'

'If you'd consider delivering, is there any chance I could persuade you to stay for a slice of pizza? There are five fourteen-year-old girls in the house — their topics of conversation range from make-up to pop stars. They're driving me mad. I'd kill for a sensible conversation.'

Pizza and conversation with a very nice man. Yes, she thought she might be able to handle that. 'I'll collect some cakes from downstairs and I'll be over as soon as I can. Where do you live?'

# Supper at Jack's

Jack replaced the phone, not sure quite what had happened. Had he really invited Paula Dixon over for supper? He hoped she wouldn't misunderstand — but it wasn't likely she'd think this was a romantic invitation. Not when Jessica and her friends were running riot through the house.

Besides, she was new in town and was sure to appreciate a friend. By all accounts, she'd spent much of her time on her own since she'd moved to Kinbrae. And too much time by oneself wasn't a good idea for anyone. Everyone needed friends.

'As requested,' she said when she arrived, handing a large cake box over. 'I hope there's enough there to keep everyone happy.'

He took the box through to the large kitchen and set it down, peering inside.

'That lot will do nicely.' He grinned and she smiled back.

She had a nice smile. And she was wearing her hair down tonight. Her hair was nice, too — glossy and thick, and he imagined it would be soft to touch.

Now, where had that thought come from?

Jack wasn't in the habit of wondering how a woman's hair would feel beneath his hand. Why was he suddenly doing so with Paula — someone he hardly knew?

He suspected he knew the reason and he didn't like it. However great Paula was — and no matter how lovely her hair — he couldn't go down that route.

It wasn't that Jack didn't want to find someone to love again. It was more that he couldn't. He had Jessica to consider. And he'd made a promise to himself that he would concentrate on raising her and making sure she was happy before thinking of what he wanted.

'Why don't you sit down,' he invited. 'I'll get the pizzas out of the oven and feed the monsters, then we can settle to our own supper.'

She pulled out a chair and sat at the kitchen table. He was aware of her eyes on him as he moved to the oven, folded tea towel in hand.

There was a shriek and loud laughter from the living room and her eyes widened. 'Are you sure there are only five of them?'

He laughed. 'Quite sure — it only sounds like there's a hundred.'

'You're very brave,' she said. 'Allowing your daughter to have so many friends over at one time. I was never allowed more than one at time.' She glanced around as another fit of loud giggling reached the kitchen from the living room. 'And we had to be quiet, at that.'

Jack was horrified. 'Children should be allowed to be noisy,' he said at last. 'It's in their job description.'

Paula smiled. 'Mum worked hard and she needed peace and quiet when she was at home.'

'What did she do?'

'She's a doctor. A GP. She still works too hard.' Paula sighed.

'I like to think I work hard, but this is Jessica's home, too. Obviously it wouldn't do to let her run riot, but it would be unfair of me to expect her to be seen and not heard.'

'I think,' she told him, her soft brown eyes settling on his face, 'that Jessica is very lucky to have such a lovely dad.'

He felt his mouth smile of its own accord and, when he felt the sudden urge to kiss his guest, he knew he was in big trouble. He turned his back to her and got busy taking the pizzas from the oven.

'I'll take these through to the girls,' he said, holding up two plates of food. 'Won't be a minute.'

The girls fell onto the food like they hadn't been fed in months, but he didn't hang around. He was very aware Paula was waiting for him in the kitchen.

'What brought you to Kinbrae?' he asked when he joined her at the table and they were tucking into their own pizza.

She paused, pizza slice midway to her mouth. 'I saw the café advertised and fell in love with it.'

'But you have no experience of running a café.'

'Is it really that obvious, do you think?'

He gave a quick shrug. 'I'm afraid it was this morning.'

'Yes.' She paused and smiled, her brown eyes bright. 'I should thank you for that.'

'You already did.'

She put her slice of pizza back on her plate and reached out to cover his hand with her own. Her hand was warm and he liked the feel of her touch.

Yes, he was in very big trouble.

'I'm seriously very grateful. I know I overreacted, but it all got a bit much and I really don't know what I'd have done if you hadn't stepped in.'

He turned his hand over so their palms were facing and his fingers curled around hers. 'You'd have been fine,' he assured her. 'I've every confidence. Anyone who can redecorate and reorganise McGregor's Café entirely on her own — and in only a few days — isn't short of coping strategies.'

Jessica and her friends were shrieking and laughing again. They'd obviously finished their meal and they sounded like a herd of baby elephants as they danced around the living room.

It seemed they'd reached the point where Jack should move and tell them to quieten down. Maybe he should even take in their cakes. But it was too comfortable sitting here in his big, untidy kitchen with Paula's hand in his. Way too comfortable.

He glanced at her lips — and again he wondered what it might be like to kiss her. In fact, he couldn't ever remembering wanting to kiss anyone more in his life.

She threw her long hair over her shoulder with her free hand and moved, just a fraction, towards him. 'Jack . . . ?'

Her voice was barely a whisper — and he liked the way she said his name. It would be so easy to lean forward, to brush his lips against hers. And what harm would one quick kiss do?

A loud crash from the living room brought him to his senses. He grabbed his hand back. 'I . . . er . . . ' he said as he tried to ignore the confusion that flashed across her face. 'It seems the monsters are running riot in there. I'd better go and see what they're up to.'

But he couldn't seem to move. What was he doing? He should never have asked Paula over. He should never have encouraged her to get cosy over pizza. It wasn't fair on her and it wasn't fair on his daughter.

Jessica had been very hurt already when the only girlfriend he'd brought into their lives had disappeared from Kinbrae. Her mother's death — well, nobody could have done anything about that. But Julie walking out on them and chasing the bright city lights . . . He'd vowed never to put Jessica through something like that again.

He might not know Paula too well yet, but he did know she was a city girl at heart. She had that city girl elegance and confidence that suggested she didn't quite belong. And, while she might have moved to Kinbrae of her own accord, she could just as easily move away again.

'You were going to see what the girls are up to,' she reminded him gently. Reluctantly, he got up and went to investigate.

'Dad, I'm sorry,' Jessica said as soon as he walked through the living room door. 'I was trying to do a handstand and I kicked the lamp over.'

Jack shook his head as he looked to where the lamp had smashed into pieces on the wooden floor. 'Honestly, how old are you lot? Four or fourteen?'

'I'm really, really sorry.' Jessica grimaced. 'We were trying out our routine for the dance competition.'

'Next time save that for when you've got more room. Now, fetch the dustpan and brush and I'll clear up this mess. Then I want you lot to calm down. You can watch a film while you eat your cakes, then you all need to get those sleeping bags out.'

✱ ✱ ✱

Paula wasn't quite sure what to do. So she sat as quietly as she could at the table, where Jack had left her.

She'd nearly kissed him. She couldn't believe it. She wasn't the kind of girl who kissed men she barely knew.

She was attracted to Jack. There was no doubt about it. And he'd proved what a lovely man he was by being so kind today when she'd been upset.

But she'd sworn off men. She'd come to Kinbrae to forget — to mend her if not quite broken, then definitely bruised, heart. Not to hurl herself headlong into another relationship. Especially when the man in question had so much going on and seemed as reluctant as she was to enter into anything romantic.

She didn't want to do anything silly. She didn't want to scare him away, not when he was her only friend in Kinbrae. And she needed him as a friend. So she'd have to ignore any awkwardness that there might be between them and pretend that something hadn't almost happened over pizza.

The door opened and a teenaged girl, long red hair flowing behind her, came charging into the kitchen. She stopped dead when she saw Paula.

'Oh.'

Paula smiled. 'Hi. You must be Jessica.'

The girl smiled. 'I didn't know Dad had company.'

'I'm Paula.'

'The lady who bought Gran's café?'

'That's right.'

Jessica's face brightened. 'Oh, good. I was hoping to get a chance to speak to you.'

Paula was surprised by how obviously pleased Jessica was to meet her, and also that the teenager was so keen to speak to her. Jessica pulled a chair out and sat next to Paula at the table.

'Dad said I wasn't to bother you at the café until you'd settled in, but I'm not doing that if you're here. Am I?'

'I suppose not.' Paula couldn't fault her logic. 'Why did you want to see me?'

'Well, you know the café's been in McGregor hands for generations.'

Paula nodded. 'I had heard.'

'And the thing is, the McGregor teenagers have all had part-time jobs there to earn extra pocket money.'

Suddenly she could see where this was heading. 'And you want to know if I'll be taking on staff?'

'Gran always promised,' she said, 'before she decided to sell up. She was going to let me work there for a couple of hours after school a night or two a week. And Saturdays.'

'That seems rather a lot for someone of your age.'

Jessica sighed. 'Well, she and Dad both said I had to wait until I was a bit older. And I'd only be allowed to carry on if I proved I didn't let my school-work slip. But then Gran sold up.'

Paula sighed. Heather had employed a couple of locals to help part-time, and neither had wanted to work for Paula. Which suited her at the moment — she'd been keen to run things herself until she got on her feet. It was to be her version of jumping in at the deep end — and she'd intended to swim. It hadn't even occurred to her that she'd have any trouble.

'I hadn't planned on taking on staff until it go a bit busier.'

Jessica gave a winning smile. 'But having a McGregor behind the counter will encourage people to visit. They expect it.'

Paula laughed, knowing Jessica's evaluation of the situation was spot-on. But she was unwilling to take advantage of a youngster's eagerness to enter the job market. 'We'll have to see what your father has to say about it,' she said.

'What her father has to say about

what?' They both turned as they heard Jack speak and he grinned in response. 'Jessica, you're not bothering Paula, I hope.'

'Of course she isn't,' Paula said, which earned a grateful smile from Jessica. Quickly, she explained the situation.

Jack shook his head. 'That was one thing when your gran had the place, Jessica, but you can't expect a stranger to take you on.'

'Paula's not a stranger,' Jessica countered. 'She's in our house and it looks like you've shared a pizza. You obviously know her. And I do, too, now we've had this little chat.'

Jack turned to Paula. 'I don't want you to feel you're in a difficult position here. If you're looking for someone to help out at some point, then we'd be very grateful if you'd consider Jessica's application. And judge it on its own merits, along with everyone else's.'

'Aw, Da-aad.' Jessica all but pouted and Paula couldn't stop herself from laughing.

'As you seem to be the only applicant, perhaps we could arrange a trial. Maybe a couple of hours tomorrow if you're free after your friends go home?'

'Really?'

'And we'll see how it goes,' Jack said. 'It's just a trial — you'll need to do a good job for Paula and prove it doesn't intrude on homework time before anyone reaches any firm decisions.' Jessica nodded enthusiastically. 'OK, I think you've put enough pressure on Paula for now.' He reached into the cupboard under the sink and took out a dustpan and brush. 'You'd better take these and get back to your friends. And sweep up that lamp before anyone gets hurt. Nobody's wearing shoes through there, and if someone cuts their feet there will be trouble.'

Jessica grabbed the dustpan and brush and bounded out of the room, no doubt planning to update her friends on this latest development. As soon as she went, Jack closed the kitchen door behind her and leaned against it, arms folded across his broad chest.

'What?' Paula asked when he didn't speak.

'You don't have to.'

'I know.'

'The café didn't come with obligations of nepotism.'

She laughed. 'I didn't for a moment suspect it did.'

'You don't need any help. So why did you say you'd employ her?'

She swallowed. His eyes were really very blue. They seemed to look right into her mind — and to see that she'd offered Jessica a job not just because she didn't want to disappoint the girl, but also because she didn't want to disappoint the girl's father.

'I'm hoping things might pick up. Besides, it's only for a few hours. And, if her father's taught her to make scones, then employing her will be an investment in the café's future.' She was babbling, but he was watching her so carefully, and when he pushed himself away from the door and took a step towards her, her mouth suddenly went dry. 'And she was right; she said it would make sense to have a McGregor behind the counter. The locals would appreciate it.'

He took another step. She got up from her chair, not knowing what she was going to do or what he was planning on doing. But knowing she needed to be on her feet.

'Paula . . . ' He was close now, and his arms dropped to his sides.

'Yes, Jack . . . ?'

She never found out what he was going to say, because Jessica chose that moment to burst back into the room, dustpan in hand. 'All cleaned up,' she said as she emptied the bits of broken lamp into the bin. 'And nobody got hurt.' She looked from her father to Paula, a big grin on her face. 'My friends are so jealous. I'm the first in our group to get a job.'

The moment was gone. His attention was on his daughter now. 'You're not working yet,' he reminded her. 'And it is only a trial, so don't go counting chickens.'

Jessica laughed. 'I'm going to make myself indispensable,' she promised as she washed her hands, then went for the box of cakes. 'Paula won't dream of sacking me once I get that trial under my belt.'

Paula laughed. She doubted her business would ever recover from the scandal if she ever sacked Heather McGregor's granddaughter from the café. But she already liked the girl and she was sure it was bound to go well.

# Settling In

Jessica arrived bright and early the next morning. 'Hi,' she called, the bell at the door still tinkling as she bounded in.

'Good morning, Jessica,' Paula replied with a smile, impressed that the girl had dressed for the part in a neat blouse and skirt, with her long red hair tied back in a pony tail. 'I wasn't expecting to see you for a few hours yet. I hope you didn't send your friends home early so you could come in here?'

Jessica laughed. 'No. Flora and Cherry are into athletics and have races this morning, and Courtney is going with her family to visit her grandmother.'

'Well I'm pleased to see you here so early,' Paula told her. 'It shows you're keen.'

Jessica nodded. 'I was so upset when Gran sold up. We all were. But Dad said she must have had her reasons.'

Family commitments was the excuse Heather McGregor had given Paula, but she wasn't about to gossip with the child. Instead, she smiled and showed Jessica where she could store the coat and the bag she'd brought with her.

There was no sign of Jack looking for his morning coffee, but it was Saturday and very likely he'd decided to have a well-deserved long lie-in. In addition, it was possible he wouldn't want to make Jessica self-conscious by turning up at his daughter's place of work on her first day.

'What can I do first?' Jessica asked.

'Wash your hands,' Paula advised. 'That's always a good start when you're going to be working around food.'

'You sound like Gran.' Jessica giggled and Paula took the remark as a compliment. Everyone thought highly of Heather, that much was obvious, so to be evaluated against her and be found equal by the other woman's granddaughter had to be a good thing. Even if it was only Paula's nagging skills that were being measured.

Over the course of the morning, Paula showed Jessica how the coffee machine worked, how to serve food hygienically, and how to use the till.

It was a quiet morning — just as Paula had predicted it would be. When a customer came and shuffled to a corner table, Jessica rushed over to take her order.

Paula stood by, her senses on red alert, waiting for trouble. However grumpy Joyce Imrie might naturally be, and however many times Paula might tolerate the woman being rude to Paula herself, there was no way she would allow Jessica to be picked on.

She needn't have worried: Joyce, if not quite the epitome of charm, was pleasant enough to the girl.

'You've done well there,' she called over to Paula as Jessica made up the order. 'I told you that McGregor's needed a real, live McGregor behind the counter.'

With those words of faint praise, Paula felt the first stirrings of hope that life in Kinbrae might turn out the way she'd hoped. Joyce was a difficult customer by any standards — Jack had made that clear. So if this very difficult customer was approving, it was one hurdle successfully negotiated.

★   ★   ★

For the first time since she'd moved here, Paula felt truly happy as she walked in the fresh air the next morning. The day was crisp and the colours were bright. Paula could see everything with a sort of clarity that had been lacking recently. It was the kind of day where it felt extra good to be alive.

She sighed softly as she listened to the clip-clopping of her own heels on the tarmac of the lane that would take her to church. Yes, moving to Kinbrae had been a good thing.

Without warning, someone grabbed her arm and she gave a start. Swinging round, she was surprised to find Jessica wearing a wide grin. 'Sorry, Paula — did I scare you?'

'A little.' She smiled. 'But not to worry. I didn't know there was anyone there, that's all.'

Jessica slipped her arm through Paula's and they began to walk along together. 'Going to church?'

'Yes.' Paula glanced down at the smart dress and jacket she kept for best. 'Yes, I am.'

'Great. You can sit with Dad and me.'

Paula was touched by the offer, but realised she needed to see what Jack had to say about it before accepting. They had been getting on so well, but she hadn't seen him since that way too comfortable Friday evening she'd spent in his kitchen. She didn't know how he would react to having her sit with them. And, if she was honest, she was a little hesitant herself — she didn't want to go down the route of spending cosy nights eating pizza with any man.

'Where is your dad?' She tried to make the question sound casual — as though the answer didn't matter much to her.

'Lagging behind.' Jessica laughed. 'I had to run to catch up with you.' She used her arm locked with Paula's to halt their progress and they both turned around to watch him approach.

Was it her imagination, or was Jack's smile a little strained? Probably her imagination, she decided as he drew level with Paula and his daughter. He was way too lovely to smile and not mean it.

*　　*　　*

Jack meant the smile — and it scared him how much he meant it. He'd only managed a day without seeing Paula before realising how much he'd missed her. He also knew that missing her so much after only one day meant he'd have to go cold turkey. Next week he'd do as his mother suggested and make use of the coffee machine in his office, rather than dropping by for a take-away drink on his way to work.

'Good to see you,' he said, while

striving to keep his expression from giving too much away. He watched, fascinated, as she smiled back at him.

'You, too. Jessica suggested I sit with you in church this morning, but I don't want to intrude.'

There was an uncomfortable silence. It wasn't that he didn't want her to sit with them — the problem was it was that he wanted it too much. 'You wouldn't be intruding,' he managed eventually. 'Please sit with us.' He was pleased Jessica was such a kind and considerate girl, but she had no idea what she was doing by bringing Paula closer to their family. Now he'd decided the only option open to him was to keep Paula at a distance, this was the last thing he needed.

He slipped into their usual pew, behind his parents and his brothers, Mark and Ryan. His family turned to greet him and his brothers raised eyebrows as they saw Paula take her seat beside him.

'His parents, thankfully, didn't betray

any surprise, by either word or facial expression. Smiling sweetly at the three of them, his mother inclined her head in greeting. And his father merely offered a hearty 'good morning'.'

Jack was aware of Paula at his side throughout the service. Next time he'd make sure Jessica sat between them so he wasn't tempted to reach out and brush her hand with his own.

Then he realised he was planning for this to happen again — for Paula to join him and his daughter on future visits to church. His jaw clenched as he rose to his feet with the rest of the congregation, ready to sing a hymn.

It didn't help that she sang like an angel. He tried to block out the sound, but it was impossible. Her voice called to him, drew him in, and he had to fight with everything he had not to give in.

Yes, the only option open to him was to avoid Paula as much as possible.

★   ★   ★

Paula blinked against the sunshine, which was a sharp contrast to the muted light inside the church. She'd liked the service and she'd liked the minister. And, looking around, it seemed that most people from town had been there today. Very unusual for this day and age.

The minister shook her hand and offered a friendly smile. 'Good to see you here today, Paula.'

Paula told him how much she'd enjoyed the service, and walked on so he could engage with the next member of his congregation.

She knew she'd had a bumpy start to her life in Kinbrae, but today she was feeling very positive. She just knew things were going to work out for her here. The one little worry today had been Jack. He hadn't looked best pleased when Jessica had asked Paula to join them. She was sure she hadn't imagined his reluctance.

'Paula.' Heather McGregor's voice sounded behind her and she turned to find the other woman beaming. 'So lovely to see you. How are things going?'

'Terrific, thank you.'

'That's good news. Listen, we're all going back to the farmhouse for lunch. Why don't you join us? Jack and Jessica are coming and my other two sons, Mark and Ryan, will be there.'

'Yes, please do.' Denny added his voice to his wife's invitation.

Paula smiled, genuinely thrilled to be asked to join the family, but she knew it was probably not a good idea. Not only was she expecting a phone call, but she guessed Jack wouldn't share his parents' enthusiasm at the thought of spending time in her company today. It was so odd — and more than a little upsetting. They had been getting on so well, and she didn't have a clue what had happened to make him suddenly so aloof towards her.

'It's very kind of you,' she said. 'But really, I have things to do this afternoon.'

'Oh.' Heather seemed disappointed. 'Some other time then, perhaps.'

★ ★ ★

When, two hours later, Paula was still waiting for her phone call, she began to wish she'd accepted the offer of lunch at the farm, regardless of whatever Jack's reaction might have been. She knew from experience that there was no point in trying to contact her mother — Nancy Dixon would be busy and was in the habit of not answering Paula's calls unless it was convenient for her to do so.

Restless and wanting to go out for a walk in the afternoon sunshine, Paula was on the verge of calling her mother anyway and leaving a message, when the phone eventually rang.

'I'm still not convinced you've done the right thing.' Nancy Dixon didn't mince her words. 'All those years at school and university wasted so you can play tea shop.'

'I'm running my own business, Mum.' Paula resisted the urge to sigh. The truth was that because she hadn't followed her mother into medicine, nothing she ever did was good enough. She was used to falling short of expectations.

'Adam came round to see me.'

Paula couldn't stop the sharp intake of breath. 'Really?' She hoped she'd managed a neutral tone. It wouldn't do to let her mother know how annoyed she still was with Adam.

'He wanted to know where you'd gone.'

Paula closed her eyes. She could well imagine the conversation between her mother and her ex-fiancé — they would have been in competition to be the most disapproving of Paula's new chosen direction.

'Well I hope you didn't tell him. I don't want him turning up on my doorstep.' Ouch — too much information. Her mother would be able to take a great deal from that and run with it. What was more, Paula very much suspected it would be brought up in future conversations.

She knew her mother loved her. But

Nancy had very definite ideas about how Paula should run her life. And it was very annoying.

'Paula, don't be so silly. Of course I told him. What's there to hide?'

'Mum, he offered me no support at all when that business blew up. What possible business is it of his where I've gone?'

There was a short silence, then she heard her mother sigh. 'You're right, of course. I'm sorry, Paula — I didn't think.'

Well, that was a first. Nancy Dixon wasn't in the habit of apologising.

'Mum, I know you're disappointed I gave up on my career, but the café's lovely,' Paula said, hoping that her mother would be in a mood to listen. 'Perhaps, when you've got time, you'd like to come and visit?'

★   ★   ★

The following days passed by way too slowly — in no small part because Jack

73

seemed to be avoiding her. On the Wednesday morning, her heart missed a beat when she spotted a tall red-haired man approaching the café. But as soon as he came in she realised her mistake — this man was younger and was wearing the scrubs of a hospital nurse.

'Hello, Ryan,' she said with a smile. 'What can I get for you?'

'A coffee, please,' Ryan replied. 'To take away.'

However much she watched the door, it seemed Jack was determined not to come in for his own morning coffee again today. She couldn't believe how much she missed him.

Things were picking up at the café, though. The first parent and baby coffee morning had gone very well. Half a dozen mums brought their children in and were pleased to have the side room to themselves.

Another area of custom that seemed to be opening up was the teenage population of Kinbrae. This happened without any intervention from Paula.

And she knew it was in no small part down to Jessica, who had told her friends that, especially with internet access, the café was a great place to go to get homework done.

It was still very early days, but the client base was growing and Paula was finding a niche for herself in town.

'What do you want to do when you leave school?' Paula asked Jessica a week after the pizza evening. Jessica was on her own with her books, her friends having disappeared to start their weekend once they'd had a drink and a snack. Paula put down the fresh orange juice she'd brought over for the girl and she sat down at the table for a moment.

Jessica's trial run the previous Saturday had gone well and, even though the girl had taken to popping in to see Paula after school, they were yet to discuss any future days for Jessica to work. Mostly that was to do with not having seen Jack this week — there was no way she'd make Jessica an offer of regular employment without clearing it with her father first.

Jessica closed her book and sat back in her chair. 'I want to do something with computers,' she said. 'Maybe be a programmer — or an IT trouble-shooter.'

'Really?' Paula couldn't hide her surprise. Jessica reminded her of herself in so many ways. 'You like computers that much?'

Jessica nodded. 'Dad thinks I spend too much time in front of the screen, but I'd be happy to be on the computer all day, if I was allowed.'

Paula was silent a moment. If that was the case, and Jack was indeed wor-ried about computer time, surely it would make more sense to have her out and about and dealing with people. Espe-cially as her trial few hours had gone so well the previous Saturday. Jack would see the sense in Jessica working here, even if it was only a few hours every weekend, Paula was sure.

'I've been meaning to talk to you about your trial day,' Paula began. Then she wondered if she should bring the matter up just yet. Jessica hadn't said anything, so perhaps she wasn't keen now she realised the reality of working at the café wasn't quite as glamorous as she'd thought. However, Jessica's expression cleared into a dazzling smile — leaving Paula in no doubt that she'd done the right thing in broaching the subject.

'I was dying to ask,' she confided. 'But Dad said I had to wait until you brought the subject up. He didn't want me to hassle you.'

Paula smiled. 'We'd need to speak to your dad,' she warned. 'I can't offer you the job unless he agrees. Saturday was a trial for you and for him as much as it was for me.'

'I'll speak to Dad.' She grinned, her eyes bright.

Paula shook her head. 'It might be better coming from me,' she said. She didn't want Jack to think she'd gone behind his back. She needed to know that he was one hundred per cent happy with any arrangement before she made any firm suggestions to Jessica.

She was pretty sure she would be able to convince him. From what she'd seen of Jessica's devotion to her books this week, her stint in the café hadn't dimmed her thirst to learn.

There was one tiny problem with her plan to speak to Jack, though — his avoidance of the café. She hadn't seen him near the place since last week.

Which suited her just fine, even if she did miss him as a friend. Because the truth was, she really didn't need the added complication of a romantic interest. Not when she needed all her energy for her business.

But, when she had something important to discuss and the man in question was staying resolutely away from her café, what was a girl to do?

Paula did the only thing she could. When she'd closed up for the day, she boxed up some of the gooey cakes from the display and she left the building.

# A Night Out

Jack wasn't answering the door.

Paula waited for a few minutes and knocked again. No, he definitely wasn't there. She looked towards where his estate car was parked in the driveway — chances were he hadn't gone far. She eyed the doorstep and wondered if she should take a seat. It might make more sense to go home and try another day, but Paula had always been the type to take action. Once she'd decided on something, she liked to do it straight away.

It did cross her mind that he might have spotted her through the window and had decided he didn't want to see her. But she quickly dismissed that notion — Jack was a grown-up and above such childish nonsense as hiding from a visitor. She was sure.

'Hello there. Looking for me?' Jack spoke from right behind her as she re-contemplated the merits of camping out on the doorstep.

Was her heart really beating a little faster just at the sound of his voice? She told herself not to be so silly. She was no daft teenager. And she'd already decided that, handsome, lovely and available or not, the red-haired Jack McGregor was not right for her. In fact, she'd decided before she'd moved here that no man at all was right for her. She didn't have time for romance — not after Adam. From now on, all she wanted to concentrate on was making a success of her new business.

She turned, her face feeling warmer. 'Hi.' She smiled. 'As a matter of fact, I was. I've brought food.' She handed the box over and he peered inside.

'Very generous. Thank you.'

She laughed. 'Not as generous as it seems. If they're not eaten today I'll have to throw them out.'

'Did you make these yourself?' he asked with a smile.

'Now Jack, don't tease — you've seen

the result of my one attempt at baking. I'm sure you know the answer to that question.'

He grinned again and, with his free hand, reached for his keys from his pocket and let them both in.

'Tea? Coffee? Something stronger . . . ?' he offered as he put the box down on the kitchen counter.

'I know this sounds odd when I've been making teas all day, but I could really murder a cup.' She sat at the table and he went to switch the kettle on and look for cups and plates.

'You're going to ruin my figure if you keep doing this,' he said as he lifted a cake each out for them both and handed her a plate.

She very nearly said something about his athletic build, but stopped herself in time. That might be construed as flirting and that would only embarrass them both. Besides, Paula didn't flirt with men any longer.

'The other one's for Jessica,' she said instead, nodding to where the box sat, the third cake still inside.

'She's at a friend's,' Jack replied. 'That's where I was just now — dropping her off. The friend's parents are taking them to a cottage up north until Sunday evening.'

'It will be nice for her to get away,' Paula said with a smile.

Jack smiled back. 'They're only going for the weekend, but her bag was so heavy I had to carry it for her.' He shook his head. 'I've no idea what she had in it.'

Paula laughed, remembering back to the teenage sleepovers and holidays she'd shared with her best friend. 'She'll need to change outfits at least a dozen times a day. And there will be shoes and make-up.'

'I clearly know nothing about the mind of a teenage girl.'

She smiled as she added milk to her tea. 'So, this is your reward for putting up with a group of noisy teenagers the other night — you have a few days to yourself.'

He nodded. 'Every now and then, the other parents reciprocate.'

Paula was suddenly mortified. He was a lone parent with rare time to spare, and here she was being a nuisance. 'I hope I'm not interrupting your plans.'

'Plans?' His blue eyes widened.

'Well, yes. I'm sure you'll have lots you want to do with Jessica away.'

He shook his head. 'Not so as you'd notice. It doesn't happen very often, so when she isn't here I'm really at a loss. If you hadn't popped by I'd probably be slumped in front of the television with a dinner for one on my lap by now.'

'You're sure I'm not being a nuisance?'

'Positive. Stay and keep me company.'

She sipped her tea, genuine warmth flowing through her veins as their eyes met over the rim of her cup. She put her drink down. 'I thought maybe I'd offended you.'

He looked startled. 'Why would you think that?'

She felt a blush spread over her face. She didn't want to sound needy and pathetic, but if she'd done something to offend him then she needed to know. 'You haven't been near the café for a week. I thought you were avoiding me.'

He averted his gaze and suddenly his own cup seemed to be the most interesting thing in the room. 'Things have been busy,' he said. He looked up and the blue of his gaze hit her full in the face. 'But I'm glad you're here now.'

She was sure he must have been busy. But she was also convinced there was more to it than that. She lifted her cake — a gooey concoction of cream and strawberries — and bit into it, more to buy time than because she was actually hungry.

'You have cream on your face.' He laughed.

Paula was mortified and searched in her pocket for a tissue, but Jack reached to the counter, picked up a roll of kitchen paper and tore a bit off. Instead of handing it to her, he leaned across the table and wiped her face.

He looked as surprised as she felt. It was worse because she didn't mind, even though she knew she should.

'Er . . . Thank you.'

'I'm sorry,' he said, putting the kitchen paper down on the table. 'I should have brought out cutlery. It's ludicrous expecting people to eat a cake like that with their hands.'

He looked so horrified by his lack of manners that she had to laugh. 'My fault entirely for bringing such messy cake.'

His answering grin had her heart beating a little faster, and she had to remind herself why she was here.

'Actually, I wanted to talk to you about Jessica.'

'What about Jessica?' He sat back in his chair. 'She mentioned she'd been doing her homework in the café. I hope she's not been bothering you.'

'Of course she hasn't. She's a lovely girl and it's a pleasure to have her pop by.' She paused, wondering how best to ask, then decided the only way was to ask straight out. 'I wondered how you'd feel about her working at the café on a permanent basis?'

He leaned back. 'You honestly think it's a good idea?'

'I do. Customers are coming back in slowly and I'm getting busier. And Jessica worked really hard last week — she was a big help.'

He raised an eyebrow.

'I haven't made her a firm offer,' Paula rushed to assure him. 'I wanted to speak to you first, to see what you thought.'

'Are you too busy to cope on your own?'

She winced. She had to be honest. 'Not yet. But it's early days. Things like the parent and baby coffee mornings are really taking off — and those customers are coming back in later in the day and bringing other friends. It's only a matter of time before I will need someone. It makes sense to have Jessica all trained up so she knows what she's doing when it does get busy. And it would do her good, too — get her out and chatting to people.'

'If you're not busy enough at the moment to need help to cope, it doesn't make good business sense to take on an assistant.'

She sighed. He was right; of course he was. But . . .

'I've spent a fortune on the place already. Paying a teenager to help me keep the place tidy for a couple of hours on a Saturday isn't going to break the bank,' she promised.

He smiled, his blue eyes crinkling at the corners. 'I'm not convinced,' he said. 'But I've heard of nothing but you and the café from my daughter for the past week. I don't think she'd ever forgive me if I ruined her chances of a permanent Saturday job.'

★  ★  ★

Jack had always known his own mind and he'd always acted decisively. But for the second Friday night in a row, he was getting cosy in his kitchen with Paula Dixon. He knew it wasn't wise — not when she was so attractive and he didn't want a relationship, but what else could he have done? Given her the box of cakes back and told her to go away? He winced at the thought — he'd never have done that, not even if he didn't like her. Which he did. Too much.

And that was the main reason why he'd stayed away from the café for the past week. Not that he could have admitted that to Paula — he knew it would have made him sound like an idiot.

'You're absolutely sure?' she asked now, her warm brown eyes alive with excitement.

'Positive. I think you might be a good influence on her.'

Paula laughed. 'Why would you think that?'

He gave an easy shrug. 'You're an independent businesswoman. You're living your own life on your own terms. That's what I hope Jessica will do.'

As he watched, a gentle blush warmed her skin and her eyes darkened. 'If you knew the truth . . . ' she began.

'What truth?' She sighed and he wished he hadn't asked. If her expression was anything to go by, it wasn't going to be good news. And he didn't want her to upset herself by raking over the past.

'When you asked why I'd bought the café when it was obvious I had no catering experience, well, I didn't tell you the whole truth.'

'You said you fell in love with it.'

'Well, that bit is true. But there's more to it.' She paused and he remained quiet, waiting for her to tell him about whatever was bothering her in her own time.

'At my last job I messed up,' she told him at last. 'Badly.'

'How did you do that, Paula?'

She sighed again. 'In my old life I was

a high flyer. I worked with computers. It was all I'd ever wanted to do — ever since I was Jessica's age. And I couldn't ever see myself doing anything else.'

'So what happened?' he asked.

'I made a mistake. I was working late, I was tired, and I cost the company I worked for a lot of money.'

'Did they sack you?'

Paula shook her head. 'No, they didn't need to. I wasn't even convinced it was my fault — the whole system crashed at first. But when we worked out what had happened, we realised it had to be me.' She shrugged. 'And I decided the honourable thing to do would be to resign.'

He shook his head. 'You ran away,' he accused softly.

'No, I didn't run away — I ran to a new life in Kinbrae. I saw this café advertised and I fell in love with it, exactly like I said. I'd been well paid my whole career. I had savings. So I was able to make a new start here.'

Suddenly the tears made sense. There

had been more to them than burnt scones. She must have been worried she'd lurched from one disastrous career to another.

'Paula.' He reached out and covered her hand with his — as she had done with him last week. And she felt every bit as good tonight as she had last week. 'If they didn't ask you to leave, then they obviously didn't blame you. So why do you blame yourself?'

'It was my fault,' she admitted. 'It cost a lot to put right. The company could have gone under.'

'It must have been horrible.'

She nodded. 'It was.'

'Then why run to a place where nobody knows you? Why didn't you stay and let your friends and family support you?'

'My best friend is newly married — in fact she's on her honeymoon as we speak. She didn't need my miserable face hanging around. My mother's way too busy to listen to me complaining. And my fiancé . . . '

There was a fiancé. Even though he

didn't see his friendship with Paula ever developing into a romance — not while Jessica was still young, in any case — he still felt a sharp pang of disappointment at this news. He drew his hand away from hers and waited for her to carry on.

She sighed again. 'My ex-fiancé,' she corrected.

And Jack all but heaved a sigh of relief.

'Adam wasn't sympathetic. We worked for the same company. He's the head of what was my department. My mistake brought the future of the entire business into question — everyone could have lost their jobs. And none of my co-workers were able to look at me after that.'

'If he loved you he would have stood by you,' Jack told her fiercely.

She nodded. 'I know that. So I guess he didn't love me.'

He reached out again and his fingers tightened around hers. 'He's an idiot.'

She laughed. 'Thank you for saying that. It's not true — he's very clever, but it makes me feel better that you'd say that to support me.'

'If that job had been your lifelong dream, why didn't you stay and fight?'

She shook her head. 'I found a new dream and I ran to that.'

She bit into her cake again and he watched, fascinated, as she ended up with cream on her nose this time. How did a grown woman manage to eat a cake and end up with cream on her nose? He shook his head and reached for the kitchen paper, tore a piece off and leaned over to wipe her nose clean.

It seemed he hadn't learnt his lesson last time and he grabbed at any excuse to touch her. She looked across at him with startled brown eyes and every thought of spending the evening on his own in front of the television suddenly left his mind.

'Do you fancy going dancing?' he asked, hoping she'd agree so he'd have a reason to hold her in his arms.

'What, now? Tonight?'

'Yes. As soon as we can get changed

into going-out clothes.'

She grinned. 'Give me half an hour.'

'It's a date,' he said. And suddenly it felt like it might be.

*   *   *

Paula couldn't believe she was getting ready to go dancing. And with Jack, of all people. But he was proving to be a good friend, and she wasn't interested in anything more — and neither, it seemed, was he. It had been pretty obvious from his casual tone that he hadn't meant this as a romantic date.

She wondered about his wife — might he still be in mourning? It was possible, and it would explain why he was still on his own after all these years. Handsome, solvent, lovely men were at a premium. If he had been looking for love, he would have been snapped up in an instant.

She found her black high-heeled sandals and slipped them on. She glanced at her reflection in the mirror and grimaced. If she'd known she was going out, she might have gone shopping. But a little black dress covered a multitude of occasions and she hoped she would pass muster.

'Gorgeous,' Jack declared with a grin when he turned up at the café to pick her up.

She was surprised to feel her cheeks growing warmer. 'You too,' she muttered, quickly averting her gaze. He was wearing dark trousers and a matching shirt — and he looked . . . well, to use his word, gorgeous.

They drove into town and Jack pulled up outside a small salsa club. 'I'd never have had you down as a salsa dancer,' she said.

'Me neither, but friends persuaded me to try and I really enjoyed it.' He glanced over at her. 'We can go somewhere else, if you'd prefer?'

'No,' she told him quickly. 'I used to go a salsa class when I was at university. I'm going to be very rusty, but if you don't mind your toes being trodden on . . .'

He laughed. 'I'm sure I'll survive. Besides, I'm probably going to be a bit rusty myself. It's years since I was last here.'

'Why did you stop coming if you thought it was fun?' She could have bitten her tongue off. What if, by 'years since', he meant he'd visited the club with his wife? Her question had been intrusive in the extreme — and she didn't know him well enough to ask such things outright. She held her breath as she waited to see if he was offended.

'Jessica,' he said with a grin that put her mind at rest. 'Good babysitters are hard to come by in Kinbrae.'

'But didn't your mother . . . ' It seemed that now she'd started with the inquisition there was no stopping her.

'Mum does a lot already. If I'd asked I'm sure she'd have agreed. But, over the years, she's always been ready to step in when I have to work. I would have felt I was taking advantage if I was always asking her to babysit so I could enjoy myself.'

Paula nodded, the realities of what it must be like for him as a lone parent slowly sinking in. 'Well now you are out, we don't want to sit out here all night,' she said. 'Shall we go in?'

The salsa beat was loud and Jack and Paula joined the other couples on the floor. It was nice being held so close. If she had been looking for another relationship, Jack would have been a serious contender.

But she wasn't.

So there was no point persisting with thoughts in that particular direction.

But, as they twirled this way and that, Paula forgot that she wasn't supposed to be falling for Jack. Something in the way he held her, and the way his blue eyes gazed at her face, made her think that he no longer saw this as a friends' outing. And that, despite the vibes he'd given off earlier, this was very much a date.

Suddenly things were deadly serious.

'Drink?' he asked when there was a lull in the music.

'Yes, please.' She grabbed at the excuse for a few minutes' break from the relentless onslaught of feelings that had very nearly overwhelmed her when she'd been in Jack's arms.

She went to sit down and he joined her a few minutes later with two cold drinks. The music had started up and was louder than ever, so it seemed entirely natural for him to sit close to her — so close that his thigh was against hers and his arm was resting along the back of her chair. How else would they each hear what the other way saying?

'This is fun,' she said.

'Yes,' he agreed. 'And you're not in the least rusty. My toes remain unbruised.'

'I thought we were both pretty good,' she said. Then she realised how big-headed she must have sounded and she laughed. And he joined in.

'We were.'

He slipped his arm from the chair to rest around her shoulders and suddenly she didn't feel like laughing any longer. She looked up into his eyes and saw he wasn't laughing now, either. 'Jack . . . ?'

He lifted his free hand and traced her lower lip with his thumb. 'You should wear your hair down more often.'

'I can't, not in the café. Food hygiene rules . . . You should know that.' She was babbling. Why was she talking about food hygiene?

He nodded. And then his head descended towards hers.

And it was unlike any other kiss Paula had ever experienced. It was sweet and strong, both at the same time. And she never wanted it to end.

But it did.

Too soon, Jack lifted his head and took his arm from her shoulder — shifting slightly so his body was angled away from hers. 'I'm sorry. I shouldn't have done that.'

Paula sat speechless for a moment. Then she realised she needed to say something. He was looking at her. Expecting some response.

'Neither should I,' she said at last. 'Jack, I'm not looking for a boyfriend. I moved to Kinbrae to get away from all that.'

'It won't happen again,' he said. 'Do you want to dance?'

She agreed. But the fun had gone out of the evening. And she couldn't help thinking it had all been her fault.

'I have a splitting headache,' she told him a short while later. 'I hate to cut the evening short, but do you mind if we leave?' Despite the unease, she wasn't keen for the evening to end, but she really was starting to feel a bit woozy and she didn't want to risk being ill in this lively club.

# Jack to the Rescue — Again

Jack knew he'd been an idiot. But the temptation to kiss Paula had been too much. If it had been only his feelings to consider, he would have gone for it, tried to persuade her that they could be a couple.

But there was Jessica. And now — with her studies and all the drama that teenage girls had to live through on the way to being grown-ups — was not the time to bring someone else into the picture. However lovely that someone else might be.

Paula had been very pale when he'd dropped her off at the café last night, so he'd allowed her to go inside quickly without holding her back. But he had to speak to her — if only to offer more assurances that he wouldn't try to kiss her again. It had been obvious from her reaction that she was as determined as he to ignore any attraction, and he didn't want to give her cause to worry.

And he needed to make sure she had recovered. Because, if he didn't, who would?

Paula had taken to opening the café early every morning, in the hope of attracting the breakfast crowd. But this morning, he noticed it was still closed as he crossed the street towards the place.

He knocked anyway. Hopefully all was well and she'd just decided to have a Saturday lie-in. Which wouldn't make him very popular, he realised, but he knocked again, just to make sure she was fine.

When she came to the door, he knew he'd been right to check up on her. She looked like death and stood pale, shivering and with a blanket draped around her shoulders.

'You look terrible,' he said. Although that wasn't quite true — she looked ill, but there was no doubt she was still gorgeous.

'Just a sniffle,' she said, and swayed unsteadily on her feet.

'A sniffle, my eye,' he muttered as she swayed again, and he caught her neatly in his arms.

'I'm fine,' she said. But it was obvious she wasn't.

'I think you need to go back to your bed.' He swept her up and headed towards the stairs that led to her tiny flat above the café.

'Jack, put me down,' she protested. 'I'm OK. Honestly. You don't need to worry about me.'

'I think we should let the doctor be the judge of that.'

'I don't need a doctor.'

'You're going back to bed and I'm calling the doctor. It's not open for debate.'

★   ★   ★

His mouth was compressed in a straight, hard line. He looked like a man who knew his mind. Even if she'd had the energy to argue, she doubted she would have won against him in this mood. She put her arms around his neck as he carried her up the stairs to her flat.

'I can't go lounging around all day. I need to open the café,' she told him weakly. 'It's Saturday. I'm hoping it will be busy.'

'You're not doing anything. Not today.' They were in her flat now and he nudged the bedroom door open and set her down. 'Back into bed,' he told her. 'I'll call the doctor.'

'But the customers have only just started to come back in. If I close up now, I'll be back to square one.' But although she had no doubt all she said was right, she still did as he had told her and got back under the covers. Quite frankly, she couldn't have stood on her own feet a moment longer.

'There's no way you can work today,' he told her gently.

Admitting defeat, she nodded.

'I'd stay and open up, only I have to go to work for a couple of hours. I'm meeting a new client and today was the only day he could make it. But leave it with me,' he said. 'I'll call Mum in. She'll be happy of a chance to spend a day behind the counter.'

'Oh, no.' She sat up too quickly and winced as a wave of dizziness assailed her. 'I don't think that's a good idea,' she said a little more quietly as she settled back against the pillows.

He looked at her with steady blue eyes, his expression giving nothing away. 'Why not?'

'Well . . . ' She really couldn't think with her head throbbing merrily. 'Well, it isn't. Heather sold the café. She obviously didn't want to work here any longer.'

'I wouldn't be so sure about that,' he said cryptically. And then he left the room.

Paula must have dozed off, because the next thing she knew, a smart young man was being shown into the room by Heather McGregor. 'This is Paula,' Heather said. 'Paula, this is Dr Carter.'

Heather left the room and the doctor

performed a quick examination. 'You've not registered at the Health Centre,' he said as he checked her temperature.

'I've only just moved to Kinbrae, Doctor. The only thing I've sorted out so far has been the café.'

He nodded. 'As soon as you're well enough to get out, it might be a good idea for you to pop in and deal with the formalities.'

'I'm hardly ever ill,' she told him by way of explanation for her neglect of something so basic. 'I didn't think I'd need a doctor.'

He shook his head. 'Nobody expects to be ill. But it's as well to be covered for such an eventuality.' She gave a cautious nod. 'Your temperature's elevated. It looks like a virus,' he diagnosed. 'Probably picked up from one of your customers.'

If she hadn't felt so poorly, she would have laughed. Just her luck that she'd caught something from her customers when those customers were still rather thin on the ground.

'Give yourself a day or two, drink lots

of fluid and, if you get any worse, call me back in.'

Heather came back in a short time after Doctor Carter had left. 'Everything OK?'

'Fine, thank you.'

'I've left Joyce in charge of the café for a few moments,' Heather confided, and Paula couldn't hide her shock. Heather laughed. 'She can be a bit abrasive, but she's OK once you get to know her,' she said. 'And she's in her element down there. She's already managed to convince three people to buy cake they didn't know they wanted.'

Paula sat up straight, dread filling her. 'Those cakes should have been thrown out this morning. I was planning to buy some new ones in.'

Heather patted her arm. 'All sorted,' she said. 'I've been baking all morning.'

Paula wondered just how long she'd been asleep. 'What time is it?'

'Lunchtime. There's a bit of a rush on down there, so I'll just serve you a quick snack and get back to it.'

'I couldn't possibly eat . . . '

But Heather had disappeared, only to come back a moment later with a tray. 'Doctor said to make sure you had plenty to drink,' she said as she loaded a bottle of water and a glass of orange juice from the tray onto Paula's bedside table. 'And, as well as baking, I've made some soup. It's going down very well with the customers. This is the last serving.'

'Just how many customers are there in the café?'

Heather smiled. 'There's at least one person sitting at every table.'

Paula sighed. She'd yet to secure even half that number of visitors at any one time. But it seemed Heather McGregor could entice customers through the door with very little effort.

'They really don't like me,' she said. It wasn't like her to feel sorry for herself, but her illness had made her feel vulnerable.

'You just need to give them time,' Heather told her with a sympathetic smile. 'The people of Kinbrae take a while to adjust to any change. But when they do, they're the most loyal and friendly bunch of people you could ever hope to meet.'

★   ★   ★

Jack's mind had been back in the café all morning. He hated that he'd had to leave Paula when she was so unwell, but he'd had no choice — he was in no more of a position to turn down possible clients than anyone else he knew.

The speed with which his mother had rushed around had astounded him. He'd phoned her, thinking he might need to do a bit of persuading, but Heather had appeared at the door practically before he'd ended the call.

Yet again, he found himself wondering exactly why his mother had seen fit to sell her business when it was pretty obvious she couldn't wait to go back. He just couldn't get rid of the feeling there was something his parents weren't telling him. Although, he recognised ruefully, he should empathise with his mother's attachment to the place, as he was finding it difficult to keep away from the café himself these days.

He wished he was in a position to woo Paula.

Everyone told him he was crazy, putting his life on hold — they said he really needed to get out there and get on with his life. But they hadn't been the ones who'd had to be there to comfort his daughter when she'd cried herself to sleep every night for months after the woman they'd all thought would be her step-mother had decided she preferred to spread her wings.

No, however much he liked Paula — and he did like her very much — there was no way he was risking Jessica's happiness again.

With a sigh, Jack picked up the phone. His mother answered her mobile within moments.

'Hey, Mum. How is she?'

'Fine,' Heather told him. 'A lot

brighter this afternoon. I think she's over the worst.'

'That's good.'

Heather was silent for a moment. An ominous silence that had Jack's nerves twitching.

'You're taking a lot of interest in Paula,' she said at last. Her tone was hopeful and he didn't like that. Understandably, perhaps, his mother didn't like the fact he was alone. Over the past few years, she'd tried to introduce him to potential girlfriends. He definitely didn't want Heather to harbour hopes in that direction where Paula was concerned. He and Paula were friends. Nothing more.

There was no romance.

But there could be, a nagging little voice in his head told him. If things had been different, there would definitely be romance.

'Stop it, Ma.'

'Stop what?' Heather's tone was now the sound of all things innocent.

'Stop trying to read more into it. You

know I'm not in the market for a girlfriend.'

'Oh, Jack. I understand why you made that decision. And I did see how upset Jessica was when Julie left. But Jessica's a sensible girl. She'll be away to university before you know it and she won't want you to be on your own.'

'Not happening, Ma.' He chuckled softly, to let her know he wasn't cross with her. Then he replaced the receiver and sat back in his black leather swivel chair.

Maybe his mother was right. Perhaps he was being overly cautious. Maybe it was time he took risks. But when he thought back to how upset his daughter had been — how much of a gap Julie had left in her young life — he knew he wasn't willing to take that much of a risk. Not where Jessica was concerned.

But, even telling himself all that, he still couldn't get Paula out of his head. He enjoyed her company. There was no getting away from it. It had been hell to stay away from the café this past week. He'd left for work knowing she was there and all he had to do was to step through the door to speak to her. And, when he'd held her in his arms as they'd danced last night — and when he'd kissed her — there had been nothing friend-like about it.

More than anything, he couldn't get over how ill she'd looked when he'd called by this morning. He was pleased his mother had stepped in, because if she hadn't, he knew he would have cancelled his meeting — regardless of what that might have meant for his company.

It was nearly three in the afternoon by the time he was finally free to head for home. With Jessica away, the first thing he did when he got back to Kinbrae was to drop by the café. Saturday was traditionally an early-ish closing at the café, and his mother was just cleaning up for the day. Jack rolled up his sleeves and got stuck in.

'I thought you were only going in to

work for a couple of hours,' she scolded.

'That was the plan. But the meeting ran on and I decided to stick around and get some stuff done.'

She shook her head. 'You work too hard.'

'Needs to be done, Ma.' He was itching to ask after Paula, but was determined to play it cool. He knew if there was cause for concern, his mother would have told him immediately.

'Thanks for stepping in today. Paula will appreciate it. She was worried about letting the customers down.'

'I'm sorry Paula's ill, of course I am,' his mother started. 'But I really enjoyed being back.'

Jack looked at her through narrowed eyes and wondered . . . She looked happier than he'd seen her for ages. 'Want to tell me the real reason you got rid of the place?' he asked.

His mother flushed a bright red. And that was when he knew beyond doubt that there was more to it than he was being told. Flustered, Heather McGregor shook her head. 'I've no idea what you're talking about,' she said, not quite meeting his eye.

He knew he couldn't press the issue. Not with Paula sitting ill upstairs and his mother keen to get home at the end of a busy day.

'OK, Mum,' he said. 'But we are going to have a proper chat soon. And you're going to have to tell me what's going on.'

His mother still couldn't quite meet his eye. 'So good to be back in the kitchen — I spent most of the morning making cakes,' she told him as she swept the wooden floor. 'I'd almost forgotten what good fun this place can be.'

And, again, he knew there was something wrong. His mother had cited the baking as one of the reasons for giving up the café. She was tired, she'd said, of making the same things day in, day out. But the woman who was in front of him now didn't look in the least weary at the thought of turning out chocolate cake upon chocolate cake . . .

Once Heather had gone, he climbed the stairs to the flat and knocked gently at the door. When there was no reply, he pushed the door open and went in. Not normally his style to invade someone's home, but what if Paula had passed out on the floor somewhere? He had to check.

She was fast asleep on the sofa. He tiptoed into her bedroom and took the duvet off the bed before returning to the sitting room to cover her up. She stirred gently in her sleep and once she settled down again, he left.

★　★　★

Paula woke at six the next morning, feeling a little stiff from her night on the sofa, but otherwise marvellous. In fact, she felt so well she even wondered if her illness had been a dream. Only the evidence that she'd slept in her living room all night proved that it hadn't been.

116

She didn't know how the duvet had arrived in the living room — Heather, she suspected — but she was very grateful. She snuggled down for a moment before carefully sitting up, in case her reclined position had given her a false sense of being recovered.

No need to worry. She felt fantastic. And she was ravenous. She quickly showered and dressed and went down to the café.

Heather was a darling. Everything was in order and a batch of cakes baked yesterday sat behind the counter, ready to be sold to a hungry public. Even Joyce Imrie couldn't find cause to complain about these, she thought with a satisfied smile.

She eyed the cakes, tempted beyond reason. But she'd barely eaten anything yesterday; she needed proper food — not sugar and fat and empty calories. However deliciously those calories were packaged, cake for breakfast wasn't a good idea.

In the kitchen she took eggs and

bacon from the fridge. Realising she'd made far too much, she was grateful when she heard gentle rapping at the door. Whoever it was, she would persuade them to join her . . . Nobody would turn down a free breakfast, would they?

Her heart skipped a beat when she saw Jack's red hair through the glass panel on the door. Her hands trembled as she did battle with the locks and let him in. She knew she should be cautious — aloof. But she owed him for yesterday: if he hadn't called Heather, the place would have stayed shut. And forcing breakfast on him seemed an appropriate way to show she was very grateful for his help.

'Hey, you.' He smiled down into her eyes. And she wished he wouldn't. It seemed far too intimate. She liked it far too much.

Even though she realised now that Adam hadn't been the love of her life, she was still upset by the lack of support from someone who had proclaimed to love her. She was emotionally bruised. And, even if she might be able to love one day, it wouldn't be any day soon. She had to remember that — even if her mouth insisted on smiling back at him and didn't respond in the slightest to her urge for caution.

'You're out and about early this morning,' she said.

'Thought I'd make the most of the morning air and go for a walk. I noticed your blinds were open, so thought I'd pop over to see how the patient is today.'

'I'm good, thank you,' she told him, still smiling up into his eyes because she couldn't help it. 'And I have to thank you for yesterday, too.'

'It was nothing.'

'You called the doctor, and your mum — and she looked after me very well.'

'It's what she does best.'

'I've made breakfast. Can you postpone your walk and join me?'

He nodded. 'Thank you, I'd like that.'

'Good.' Her smile was making her

jaw ache, but she just couldn't stop. 'Why don't you take a seat and I'll bring it through.'

* * *

They sat at the window, in full view of the entire village at this early hour — with the café officially shut — and enjoyed a leisurely Sunday morning breakfast.

And Jack couldn't remember when he'd felt happier. She was so easy just to be with — talking and spending time in her company was fast becoming his favourite pastime. 'It's good to see you looking so much better,' he said. 'You gave me quite a fright yesterday.'

She blushed a delightful red and he smiled. 'I didn't mean to throw myself at you like that. But thank you for breaking my fall.'

'My pleasure.' There was a lot of smiling going on this morning and he made a concerted effort to keep his face straight. 'I need to talk to you, Paula.

About the other night.'

'The kiss?' she asked, looking awkward.

'Yes, the kiss.'

She sighed, and her gaze met his. Despite everything his head told him about it being a bad idea, when she looked at him like that his heart urged him to go for it.

'Jack, it was a lovely kiss. And, if I was going to kiss anyone again, it would definitely be you . . . '

'But . . . ?'

'I meant what I said the other night. I'm not looking for a relationship.'

He sighed. Neither was he, he'd decided. But even though he knew it was for the best, to have her give him the brush-off like this still hurt.

'We can still be friends, though?' he suggested.

She smiled again and he breathed a sigh of relief. To lose her as a friend as well would have been unbearable. And, at least this way he didn't have to explain to her about how much Julie leaving had hurt Jessica. Or that he couldn't risk bringing another woman into their lives because of that.

At least he didn't have to be the one to turn her down.

'When does Jessica get back?' she asked inbetween eating mouthfuls of bacon and egg.

'By teatime.'

Paula nodded. 'I might ask her if she wants to do a few hours at the café next weekend. If that's OK with you?'

'It's fine. You don't need to worry; I'm not going to change my mind. You've convinced me it will do her good.'

She smiled. 'Good. I'm looking forward to the company.'

'Business is picking up, though, isn't it?'

'It is,' she said. 'I've had some people in over the past few days. And trade was back to normal yesterday.'

'Mum,' he said.

Paula nodded. 'She did fabulously well. Worked so hard. I can't begin to thank you for asking her to come in and take over. And I don't know how on earth I'm going to thank her for all the work she did.'

'No need for thanks. That's what friends do — they help each other out.'

# Employing a Cake Maker

It was all very well Jack saying there was no need for thanks, but Paula knew she owed a big debt to both him and his mother. She'd deal with him later, but for now, she knew she needed to convey to Heather exactly how grateful she was for her help. The least she could do was pay her for her time. And flowers would probably be a good idea, too — for stepping in at such short notice.

With no florist in Kinbrae, she got a bouquet of hand-tied lilies delivered to McGregor's café on Monday. She would have had them delivered to the farmhouse where Heather and Denny lived, but she wanted to take them personally after she'd closed up for the day. Anything less would have been rude.

'Paula,' Heather greeted. 'How are you today?'

'I'm much better — thanks to your expert care.'

'All I did was bring you a couple of drinks.'

'And you looked after the café so I didn't have to worry. I've brought you these to say thank you.'

Heather took the bouquet from her and breathed in the scent. 'Oh, how lovely. But there really was no need. Do you have time to come in for a cup of tea?'

She followed Heather into the large farmhouse kitchen and sat at the scrubbed wooden table. 'I brought you this, too.' She slid a white envelope into Heather's hand.

'What is it?'

'Wages.'

Heather looked mortified and Paula wondered briefly if she was doing the right thing in paying up. But of course she was, she told herself sternly. Heather had done a fantastic job yesterday. She deserved to be paid.

'I really can't take this,' she said,

trying to hand the envelope back.

'Yes you can. You earned it.' She could see the other woman wasn't convinced. 'Please,' she said. 'I really would be happier if we kept things straight.'

Reluctantly, Heather put the envelope on the sideboard. 'Thank you,' she said. 'I didn't come down to help because I expected you to pay me. But there's no doubting it will be handy.' She sat at the table next to Paula and covered her face with her hands.

Paula sat stock-still, wondering what was happening. When Heather still hadn't moved after several minutes, she tentatively put a hand on the older woman's arm. 'What is it? Can I help?'

Heather allowed her hands to drop to her lap. 'Jack doesn't know. We couldn't bring ourselves to tell any of the boys. But Denny's company's in trouble.'

Paula frowned. 'It's a haulage business, isn't it?'

'That's right. We have specialist lorries to carry computers and high-tech equipment. But things have been slow.

And then we had to replace a couple of the vehicles . . . '

Paula wasn't daft. She knew how costs could mount up in a business if you weren't careful. That was the main reason she'd done the decorating in the café herself.

'Running a business can be expensive.'

Heather nodded. 'Sometimes I wish we hadn't given up on the farming. We rent the land out to a neighbour now,' she explained. 'But things were going so well with the haulage business, and it seemed daft to try to do both.'

'That's why you sold the café,' Paula said, suddenly realising.

'It is. Jack's suspicious. He knows I love that place. But if we'd told him what had happened he would have insisted on helping.'

'And would that have been so bad?'

Heather sighed. 'Denny would never have allowed it. He's a proud man. He would never accept financial help from any of our children.'

'But he let you sell the café.'

'That was different. I convinced him that as it had come to us from his mother, then he wouldn't be accepting charity. Morally, it was already his.'

Paula nodded. She could follow that logic — even though it made her sad that Heather had lost her café. 'But if Jack can afford to help, you could have kept the café . . . '

'Denny build his business up from nothing. It means a lot to him to be able to stand on his own two feet.'

Again, Paula could understand that. 'So, might you be looking for a job?' she asked Heather.

Heather took a deep breath. 'At the café?'

'Well, maybe not at the café exactly, not yet at least. But you know I'm having to buy cakes from the bakery in town? Jack told me I'd be hard pressed to make a profit doing it that way, and he was right. So what I was wondering was, would you be interested in providing the café with some of your scrummy baking?'

Heather's grin wiped the last remnants of doubt from Paula's mind. This was the right thing to do. 'You could say I'd be interested,' Heather said. 'You could also say I'm about ready to snatch your hand off . . . Thank you so much, Paula. You can't have any idea how much this means.'

Paula laughed. 'You can't know how much it means to me and the community to know there will be genuine McGregor baking on offer in the café again.'

'Speaking of McGregors at the café,' Heather continued, 'Jack tells me my granddaughter is going to be helping out?'

'She did a few trial hours the other day,' Paula said. 'Jack's fine with making it a permanent thing, so I'll speak to her when she pops in next.' Then Paula remembered how concerned everyone was that the job didn't impact on Jessica's schoolwork. 'It would only be for a couple of hours a week,' she rushed to reassure. 'And I wouldn't expect her to do too much. Taking orders, delivering teas to the tables, maybe a bit of clearing up . . . '

Heather laughed. 'You don't need to convince me. I think it's a fantastic idea. No doubt you've been told that, including my boys, four generations of McGregors have worked in that place?'

Paula nodded.

'And it will be nice to see a fifth,' Heather said.

'Especially now you're officially back on the books, too.'

'Yes,' Heather agreed. 'Especially with that.' She grinned again, then reached out and squeezed Paula's arm. 'Thank you so much, dear,' she said. 'I'll make sure you don't regret it.'

'I know you will.' Paula smiled. And she hoped she might be in a position soon to employ Heather to work in the café a few hours a week. But she didn't say so, not yet. They'd need to see how things went. Although she was pretty sure that now they'd have genuine McGregor baking on offer again, the locals would come flooding back.

'Now,' Heather said, getting to her feet, 'let me see about that cup of tea. And I tried a new recipe for a strawberry gateau today — will you try a piece to see if it's something we could maybe offer customers at the café?

★　★　★

Paula was pleased Heather McGregor had agreed to provide baking for the café. And she was flattered the older woman had confided in her about Denny McGregor's business worries. But she was deeply uneasy that she'd been asked to keep the information from Jack. It didn't see right, somehow. She knew Jack would want to know.

And she felt a certain loyalty to Jack. He had been the first person in Kinbrae to befriend her. And he had gone out of his way to help her — even when performing those good turns meant he was late for his own work.

So being asked to keep this from him

made her feel she was betraying him in some way. But she'd given Heather her word, so what could she do?

Jack was waiting on her doorstep when she arrived home and she made an effort to put the matter from her mind for now.

He grinned as she got out of her car and walked towards him. 'Hello,' he said.

'Hi there. This is a nice surprise.' And it was.

'I have another night of freedom,' he told her with a mock grimace. 'Jessica's staying with her friend overnight because they need to get to school early tomorrow. There's a school trip and the bus leaves at 7.30. Her friend's mum is going to run them both in. So, I wondered if you fancied doing something?'

She smiled. 'That would be nice. What did you have in mind?'

'Dinner and a film? If you don't mind a drive into Aberbrig.'

'I'd love that,' she said. 'Give me a second and I'll go and grab my handbag.'

A non-date doing date-like things with a lovely man who understood she didn't want a relationship. That was fine, she told herself.

But as she sat in the passenger seat of his car, she did wonder . . . If she'd met him at a different stage in her life, and if her confidence hadn't been dented before she'd arrived in Kinbrae, perhaps she might have been inclined to explore the attraction between them.

★   ★   ★

It had seemed like such a good idea to Jack — to invite this woman who didn't want a romantic relationship on a night out. That was a safe option, surely. Nobody was going to get hurt. And they were just friends.

But Jack caught himself thinking, when he least expected it, that Paula would make a rather lovely girlfriend.

'Did Jessica have a nice time with her friend at the weekend?' Paula asked as the countryside whizzed by.

'She seems to have enjoyed herself. And given I only got a text — singular — I'm guessing that means she was having too good a time to worry about her old dad.'

Paula giggled. 'That's teenagers for you.'

'I wouldn't have it any other way, though,' he said. 'As long as she's happy, then I'm happy.'

At his side, Paula nodded. Although he doubted she truly understood. Friends who had no children of their own rarely did.

She gave a soft sigh. 'Jessica's very lucky to have a dad like you.'

This was the second time she'd made such a comment. He glanced over. Her expression gave nothing away.

'Are you speaking from experience?'

'You could say. My dad died in an accident at work before I was born. I never even met him — but I still miss him.'

'I'm sorry. So it was just you and your mum?'

'Yes. I think that was why Mum spent

so much time at work — she was grieving for Dad and it was easier to forget if she kept busy.'

'And what happened to you when she was at work?'

'When I was young, we had a succession of nannies and au pairs.'

'A succession?'

She laughed. 'Mum can be difficult. I love her, but she's not the easiest person to get on with sometimes.'

'She fell out with your nannies?'

'There were . . . differences of opinions.'

His heart went out to her. It seemed her childhood had been a lonely one — something he couldn't imagine, having grown up with a house full to bursting with brothers and parents. And, even though he was on his own with Jessica, she was surrounded by loving family members — grandparents, uncles . . . and of course, Jack himself spent as much time as he could with his daughter.

There wasn't long before the film, so

they stopped for a quick meal in a tiny restaurant. 'I could have made us something at the café before we left,' Paula said.

Jack shook his head. 'That wouldn't have been a night out.'

'True,' she agreed. 'But it would have made sense as we don't have much time.'

'Perhaps you can cook something next time,' he suggested. He was pleased when she didn't disabuse him of the notion that there might be a next time.

The film, a comedy, had them both laughing. It was good to laugh — and ever better to laugh along with Paula.

'That was great,' she said as they walked back to the car. 'I'm so glad you invited me.'

'We'll need to do it again,' he said, then frowned. She wasn't looking to date anyone, he reminded himself. And neither was he. It seemed he was having to remind himself of that a lot around Paula.

'That's a good idea,' she said. They

were at the car now and he found the keys in his pocket. As he pressed the remote button to unlock the car, she stood on tip-toe and pressed her lips against his. Her kiss was brief — too brief — but it was enough to have his heart racing.

It seemed she'd forgotten her own no-dating rule, too. Her eyes widened in surprise as she looked up at him. 'I don't know why I did that,' she muttered, confused. Then she sighed and leaned towards him ever so slightly in an unmistakeable gesture of encouragement. Unable to resist, he gathered her in his arms and, as his head descended towards hers, all rational thought of this not being a good idea suddenly evaporated. And, when her arms came up around his neck, and she ran her fingers through his hair, he realised that trying to be friends with Paula Dixon was definitely a very daft idea indeed.

As they drove down the dark country road home to Kinbrae, Paula was very quiet. So was Jack. Though he felt he should say something. Something that would bridge the silence between them.

But of course, there was still Jessica and her feelings to take into consideration. And there was still Julie, who had broken his daughter's heart — even if she hadn't quite broken his. There weren't any words that would overcome those reasons for staying just friends. Or, if there were, Jack couldn't think of them at the moment.

'Jack, stop. Look — what's that?'

He noticed the same moment she spoke. Something caught in the powerful beam of his headlight. Something in a heap at the side of the road a little way up ahead.

An animal? Or a human?

He came to an immediate stop and they each threw open their respective doors and got out.

# Rescuing Joyce Imrie

They both ran to the spot that was illuminated by the car's powerful full beam. Paula recognised the heap's coat. 'Joyce?' she asked.

'Mmmmm,' the heap replied.

Jack got to his knees. 'Joyce, what happened? Are you all right? What are you doing out here at this time of night?'

Joyce stirred and sat up, looking horribly shaken. 'I was riding a bicycle. I think I must have hit a pothole or something.'

'I thought you'd been knocked over by a car,' Paula said, and was quickly offered a scathing look from Joyce. 'Not that hitting a pothole isn't bad enough,' she hurriedly added.

Slightly placated, Joyce looked around. 'Is the bike OK?'

It was only then that Paula noticed the bicycle that was lying a short distance away. 'Never mind the bike,' she said. 'The main thing is, are you OK? I think we should phone for an ambulance.'

'Nonsense,' Joyce insisted, struggling to her feet with Jack's help. 'I'm perfectly fine. Thank you for stopping, but I'll just get back on the bike — I need to get home. Cleo needs to be fed.'

'Cleo?' Paula asked faintly.

'Joyce's cat,' Jack supplied. And then he turned to Joyce. 'You're not cycling anywhere at this time of night. And especially not after you've taken a fall.'

'I'm fine, honestly. There's no need for all this fuss.'

'We happen to disagree,' Paula said. 'Even if you feel fine now, you're bound to be shaken.'

'And we'll get Dr Carter to have a look at you when we get you home,' Jack added.

'Don't be silly. We can't possibly bother the doctor at this time of night. Is the bike OK, do you think?' she asked again, more anxiously this time. And just the mere fact she seemed more concerned for a bit of metal than she did for her own health had Paula convinced the older woman was suffering from shock.

'It looks fine,' Jack told her as he lifted it into the back of his estate car.

'It's my sister's,' Joyce confided. 'I'd never forgive myself if I'd damaged it.'

'I'm sure your sister will be more concerned about you,' Paula said as she helped Joyce to the car.

Joyce laughed. 'You don't know my sister. She rides that bike everywhere.'

'Paula might not know Alice, but I do. And I know she won't be worried about the bike. What were you doing out on the road at this time of night?'

'I'd been to visit Alice — my sister,' she added for Paula's benefit. 'And we were chatting and forgot the time. I missed the last bus so she said I could borrow her bike.'

He shook his head. 'So you thought it would be a good idea to cycle along this road in the dark?'

'Why didn't you stay with your sister for the night?' Paula asked. 'You could have come home on the first bus in the morning.'

'Cleo,' Joyce replied.

And Paula realised she would have probably done the same and cycled home if she'd been responsible for a pet.

They were back in Kinbrae in no time. Jack unloaded the bike and Paula helped Joyce into the house. Despite the woman's protestations to the contrary, she was in obvious pain — wincing with every step.

'Jack, I think you were right, we should call Dr Carter,' Paula called over her shoulder.

'No,' Joyce insisted. 'I've already said.'

'I'm afraid you don't have a choice,' Jack told her, as he pulled his mobile from his pocket. 'We can't leave you like this without making sure there's nothing worse than cuts and bruises.'

Reluctantly, Joyce nodded. 'Well, if

you insist. But I'm not happy about it.'

'Your objections are noted,' Jack told her as he dialled the doctor's number.

Dr Carter was over within minutes and examined the patient in the living room, while Paula and Jack waited for the verdict in the kitchen. He appeared a short while later.

'She's in shock,' he said.

'I thought so,' Paula replied. 'You can't take a fall like that in the dark and not have a big fright.'

'I don't think she should be alone tonight,' the doctor added. 'Would either of you be able to stay with her? Just to offer reassurance if she needs it?'

Paula looked at Jack, horrified. She knew Joyce probably wouldn't, as a single woman on her own, want Jack to stay. Which left Paula herself. But she and Joyce hadn't exactly hit it off . . . Would the older woman want Paula invading her home?

'It would only be to provide tea and sympathy for one night,' the doctor added. 'There's a spare bedroom, I understand. And I've advised her to have a cup of tea and take a couple of painkillers — but she mentioned she would sleep easier knowing there was someone here if needed.'

Paula nodded. 'Of course I'll stay,' she said. 'As long as Joyce doesn't mind.'

Dr Carter smiled at Paula. 'Thank you,' he said. 'Joyce will appreciate your help.'

'I take it you're fully recovered?' he asked Paula.

'I'm fine, Doctor. Thank you.'

'Good. Well, don't forget to get yourself registered at the surgery when you have a minute.'

Paula put the kettle on so she could make the tea that the doctor had advised, while Jack saw him out.

It was proof, if proof were needed, that Joyce was indeed badly shaken, when she didn't try to argue against the case for Paula staying over to keep an eye on her. Sitting subdued in her chair, she allowed the tea to be poured and accepted the drink Jack handed to her.

'That's very kind of you, dear,' she said, sipping the hot, sweet liquid. Paula caught Jack's glance and he gave a little frown.

'Ring me if you're worried. Whatever time it is,' he told her in a quiet voice as she went to see him out.

'We'll be fine, don't worry,' Paula said, and she offered a reassuring smile.

The phone started to ring as she went back into the living room to join the patient. Joyce reached out to where it sat on a side table and picked up the receiver. 'Alice!' she exclaimed. 'I was just about to phone you to let you know I was home.' And then she promptly burst into tears.

With a sigh, Paula took the receiver from Joyce's cold hand. She introduced herself and explained what had happened. 'Your sister's fine,' she assured. 'Just a bit shaken, which is understandable. A good night's sleep should see her right.'

'I'll get the first bus over in the

morning,' Alice said, with a concerned wobble in her voice.

Joyce's sister Alice arrived about half an hour before Paula needed to leave to open up the café. Not that she would have left if Alice hadn't arrived — there was no way she would have abandoned Joyce when the woman was still in need of company.

Paula did a double take when she opened the door to the woman.

Alice smiled. 'We're twins,' she said. 'Identical.'

Although there were subtle differences — Alice seemed softer, kinder . . . And those qualities showed in her face. Paula really couldn't imagine Alice ever being cross about a damaged bicycle, as Joyce had hinted she might be.

'Joyce was up half the night talking about the accident,' Paula told Alice. 'But she eventually settled down. And she was still asleep when I checked on her ten minutes ago.'

'It was so good of you to stay with

her last night,' Alice said, taking off her coat and moving to put the kettle on.

'Not at all — anyone would have done the same. Why don't you sit; you've had an early start. I'll make us both a cup of tea before I go and open up the café.'

★  ★  ★

Jack hadn't slept much, and it showed in the extra lines around his eyes and the deeper grooves between mouth and nose. Just as well he wasn't too bothered about his looks. He grinned as he looked away from the bathroom mirror and ran a quick comb through his hair.

He'd hated leaving Paula with the responsibility for a shocked and bruised Joyce Imrie. And he'd been especially aware that the woman's hostile manner had already upset Paula on a previous occasion. But equally, it hadn't been a possibility to leave Joyce on her own. The woman had obviously been shaken by her experience, and he knew Paula would be a kind and caring companion to anyone in that situation. He didn't know how he knew; he just did. Something about her nature spoke to him on a deep level. And that made him uncomfortable in so many ways. But it also made him feel he'd known her forever.

He saw the café was open as he drove past on his way to work, and he pulled in so he could see how she was.

'Coffee?' she asked as he came through the door. 'Oh, you look shattered.'

'I'm fine,' he said, because if he admitted to his sleepless night, she might well ask the reason. And he really didn't want to tell her that thoughts of her had kept him awake. 'How's Joyce?' he asked.

'She's OK. She woke just before I left. Her sister Alice arrived on the first bus this morning, so I thought it would be fine to come over here and open up.'

'I thought you might phone me,' he said. 'I looked across at two and the lights seemed to be on.'

'Joyce couldn't sleep for ages, so I sat up with her.'

'You should have phoned me.'

'I thought about it.' She smiled and his breath caught. How did she do that — a tiny, friendly gesture and it made him want to grin back like a lunatic. Even though he was exhausted.

Through force of will, he controlled his facial muscles and retained what he hoped was a sensible expression. 'I'd best get off to work.' He picked up the take-away coffee cup from where she'd put it on the counter for him and dug in his pocket for money . . . but she put her hand on his arm.

'Jack,' she said softly. 'I think you know by now that providing you with your breakfast coffee is my pleasure.'

Her eyes were dark and there was a hint of a smile on her lips. He found he lost all control of his facial muscles at that point and they broke into an unrestrained smile.

He thought about Paula on his way

to work and while he sat at his desk, supposedly going through the piles of papers waiting for his attention. 'This is ludicrous,' he said to himself, pushing the papers to one side. He needed to get a grip.

Either he needed to ask her out properly, or he needed to stop seeing her completely. Being just friends wasn't working. At least not for him.

But the reason for not pursing the obvious attraction between them still remained. Jessica was his priority. Bringing another woman into their lives wasn't just going to affect him. And then there was the fact Paula didn't want a relationship . . .

But, whenever she looked at him, her eyes told a different story. And, when she'd kissed him last night, it was exactly as a woman who did want a relationship might have done.

Jessica was due home from her school trip at four, and he would leave work early to meet her, he decided. And he was going to have a chat with her.

His daughter wasn't a baby any longer. She was fourteen — growing up way too fast. He was going to ask her what she thought about Paula — and see how she would feel if he asked her out. And he was going to gently explain that it wouldn't necessarily mean he and Paula would be getting married. Just so she didn't get her hopes up like she did the last time he'd dated.

Surely Jessica was old enough now to understand that two people could like each other and want to spend some time together without it leading to the three of them being a family.

★　★　★

The café was busier than Paula had ever seen it. Even though it wasn't the designated day, the parent and toddler group arrived to make use of the second room. And others popped in, having heard of Joyce's accident — and of Paula and Jack's part in the drama. Everyone, it seemed, wanted to hear about the rescue first-hand.

Paula could have cried with gratitude when Heather McGregor turned up a little way into the morning. 'I don't suppose you're free to help out for a couple of hours?' Paula asked with a pleading little smile.

Heather grinned. 'Of course I am.' She put her delivery of cake boxes down on the counter, slipped off her coat and picked up a spare apron from behind the counter. 'You get these cakes sorted — make sure you're happy with everything. And I'll make a start on reducing this queue to manageable proportions.'

Paula didn't know how she'd have managed without Heather's help. And, when the lunchtime rush quietened down, she told her so.

Heather laughed. 'I've really enjoyed it,' she said.

'Enough to think about coming back part-time?' Paula asked. She hadn't planned on asking; it just slipped out. But now the offer was out there, she knew it made sense. She needed Heather. And, by the sounds of it, Heather needed the café.

Heather's grin spoke volumes. 'Do you really need to ask?'

By the time Jessica flew through the door, her blue eyes bright, red ponytail flying out behind her, the lunchtime rush was just a distant memory and only a couple of tables were still occupied. 'We're back from the trip earlier than we thought and Dad's not home from work yet,' she said, sitting down at the table nearest the counter.

'Hello, darling.' Heather took over a glass of orange juice and piece of fruitcake and gave her granddaughter a quick cuddle while she was there. 'Did you have a nice time?'

Jessica nodded. 'It was fab. What are you doing here, Gran?'

'Helping out — isn't it obvious?'

Jessica frowned and glanced over at Paula. Paula could see she was worried about what might happen to the hours Paula had promised her. But, to the girl's credit, she recovered quickly and smiled at her grandmother. 'It's great to see you back behind the counter.'

'Thank you, sweetheart. It's great to be here.'

'Actually, Jessica,' Paula said, 'I wonder if you're free for a moment. I'd like a word.' And she led the girl into the now-empty second room and they sat down at a table.

'What's wrong?' Jessica asked, eyes wide.

'Nothing at all.' Paula smiled kindly. 'Quite the opposite, in fact. I was speaking to your dad and he says it's OK if we wanted to make your hours permanent. We can work out something that suits us both — but only if you want . . .'

Jessica whooped with delight, threw her chair back and came around the table to give Paula a hug. 'That's fantastic!' she cried. 'Oh, thank you. Thank you so much. I can't wait to tell everyone.' And with that, she flew out of the door.

Paula looked across to Heather — who

lifted an eyebrow — and then they both burst into spontaneous laughter.

Heather left shortly after that — it had gone very quiet in the café and Paula would be closing up soon, so there seemed no point in her hanging on. 'We can talk about when you'll need me next when I bring the cake delivery tomorrow,' she said as she left. Paula was very grateful that she would have Heather's experience and talent to rely on.

She was wiping the tables when Joyce and Alice came in. 'Good evening, ladies.' She smiled, happy to see them, but at the same time she braced herself for Joyce's caustic tongue. She secretly hoped it would make an appearance, because that would prove the woman was her old self.

'Are we too late for tea and cake, dear?' Alice asked Paula.

'Of course not. Take a seat, please.'

Joyce smiled — and Paula was worried because that smile proved the woman she'd got to know was still not back to normal after her fall.

Paula brought the tea and cakes the ladies had ordered, then went back behind the counter to start her day-end routine of tidying and cashing up. She looked up in mild surprise as the bell went, indicating another customer had walked through the door.

'Good evening, Dr Carter.' She smiled. 'What can I get for you?'

'Oh, nothing, thank you. I wouldn't want to bother you at this time of day — not when I can see you're getting ready to close up. But I saw Alice and Joyce were here, so I had to pop in to see how things were.'

As he walked over to the table, Alice pushed out a chair for him to join them. 'Good evening, Doctor,' she greeted. 'Please sit with us.'

Deciding it was just as much trouble to clean up after three as two, Paula took an extra cup over to the table and Alice obliged by pouring the doctor some tea.

'Still have those laptops in here, I

see,' Joyce commented before Paula could go back to her tidying up.

'Er . . . ' Paula looked from the doctor to Alice. The disapproval on Joyce's face proved loud and clear that she had suffered no permanent damage from her accident. She was very definitely back to normal. 'Yes, I have.'

Joyce shook her head and it looked as though she was about to say something else, when the buzzing of Paula's mobile from behind the counter gave her the excuse she needed.

'Excuse me — I'd better get that,' she told them with a smile.

# Information Technology

Her smile deepened when she glanced at the display and saw who it was. 'Hello, Mrs Brown,' she said. 'How was Hawaii?'

Her friend sighed down the line. 'Just fab. The best honeymoon ever.'

Paula laughed. 'Well a honeymoon is once in a lifetime, so I should hope so. When did you get back?'

'We're in the taxi driving from the airport now.'

'You've phoned me and you're not even home yet?'

'Thing is, we have some time,' Ellie said. 'A few days before we go back to work. And we both want to see your new café.'

'Seriously?' Paula could have cried. Yes, the local people were starting to accept she was in charge of the café now. Yes, she had made at least one good friend in the area. But the thought of seeing Ellie's and Andrew's familiar faces made her so happy.

'Everything all right, dear?' Alice asked as she approached the counter with her purse.

'Terrific, thank you.' Paula gave a loud sniff. 'I'm just being silly. That was my best friend — she and her husband are going to visit the café.'

'All the way from London?'

Paula nodded. 'They're only just back from honeymoon, so it means a lot that they're willing to drive all this way just to visit me.'

Alice smiled. 'Of course they'll want to see for themselves that you're happy and settled in. Joyce was telling me how brave you've been, moving all this way to run your own business by yourself.'

Paula felt her eyes narrow as she glanced across to where Joyce sat poker-faced beside her smiling sister and the doctor.

'She did?'

'Yes, she did,' Alice confirmed.

'People are very impressed with you, you know.'

Paula was convinced Alice was only being nice, but she smiled in response. 'That's very kind of you to say.'

★ ★ ★

Jack had a feeling things weren't going to go well when the computer refused to boot up the next morning.

Claire appeared at his office door, face flushed, a frown on her face. 'They're all down,' she said. 'It must be the server or something.'

He sat back in his chair and let his breath out in a long hiss. 'I don't believe this.'

Claire stepped cautiously into the room and sat on at the chair on the other side of his desk. 'You still haven't found anyone to replace Derek, have you?'

He ran a rough hand through his hair. 'No. Not yet.'

Claire bit her lip. 'What are we going to do?'

He shook his head. He was good at what he did — very good. And he could use the programmes he needed as a professional. But he knew nothing about computers when they went wrong.

'I'll sort something out. Don't worry.' Said with more confidence than he felt. He didn't like to admit that he'd dropped the ball with this. Jack was accustomed to getting things right and covering every eventuality. And, if the server was down, he and his employees would be held up, which could only impact negatively on his clients.

His mobile rang. With another heavy sigh, he reached to where it sat on his desk. The display showed it was Jessica. If it had been anyone else he would have ignored it.

'Hey sweetheart. What's wrong?'

'Nothing.'

'Then why are you ringing me in the middle of a school day? I thought they had rules about things like that.'

'Oh Dad, nobody actually pays any attention to that rule.' She laughed.

'Besides, it's lunchtime.'

Mildly surprised, he glanced at his watch and saw she was right. A morning of work missed already. He really would have to sort the computer thing out soon, before more time was wasted. But first he needed to know why Jessica had called.

'What can I do for you?'

He heard her giggle as he referenced the fact she only ever seemed to phone when she wanted something. 'Katie's asked if I can go round to hers after school. We want to work on a history project.'

'I don't see why not,' he said. Katie lived here in Aberbrig, which wasn't a huge problem, but it would mean Jessica would miss the school bus home. 'Give me a ring when you're ready to leave and I'll drive round to get you.'

'Thanks. Is everything OK with you? You sound a bit stressed.'

Oh dear. And he'd tried to hide it so well. 'Computer problems,' he said.

'Anything I can help with?'

'It's the server. It's gone down and nobody knows what to do about it.'

There was a short silence from the other end. And then she spoke. 'Have you thought of Paula?'

Of course he'd thought of Paula — he'd thought about her a lot. But he knew that wasn't what his daughter meant. He closed his eyes and remembered how upset Paula had been when she'd told him about what had happened in her old life.

'I can't ask her, Jessica. It wouldn't be fair.'

'She knows all about computers, Dad. I was talking to her at the café the other day and . . . '

'Jessica, I said no,' he insisted. He wasn't about to tell his teenage daughter Paula's secret. But she had to understand that involving Paula wasn't an option. No matter how desperate he was. He'd seen the haunted look in Paula's eyes as she spoke of her old job. There was no doubt that the experience had hurt her badly. He didn't want to be responsible for bringing those sorts of memories back for her.

'What are you going to do then, Dad?'

He had absolutely no idea as things stood. 'I'll sort it,' he said, and was pleased he again sounded a heap more confident than he felt. 'In any case, you don't need to worry.'

He was on the phone trying to find someone to help when his door burst open and Claire came in, closely followed by Paula.

He put the receiver down. 'What's going on?'

'I might ask you the same thing,' Paula said. 'Why didn't you phone me?'

He shook his head. 'Jessica told you.'

'She did. And thank goodness one of you had the good sense to involve me. Why didn't you call? Did you think I'd refuse to help?'

He grimaced. 'I thought I might find someone who would step in.'

Claire shook her head. 'This is a

small town, with only even smaller towns and villages for miles around. You know that Derek emigrating to Australia has left a huge gap in the market. Anyone else who's in that line of work and close enough to help at short notice is rushed off their feet.'

'I've been made aware of that,' he said. But he wasn't annoyed with Claire. How could he be annoyed about anything when Paula had rushed to help him? 'But I'll find someone. I'm sorting it . . . ' he said. Then he glanced at Paula, not wanting to say too much while his assistant was within earshot, but the truth of the matter was that he didn't want to upset her.

Paula shook her head, a gentle smile about her mouth. 'Oh, Jack. You are a silly boy.'

And he laughed, because nobody had called him that for twenty years. And even then it had been his mother. 'I suppose I am.'

'You didn't call me because you were worried I'd make a mess of your system,' she accused softly.

'No. Of course I don't think that.'

She shrugged. 'I might in your position. After all, you've seen how hopeless I can be in the café. And I told you why I left my job in London.'

He didn't say anything. He didn't know what would be the right thing to say.

'I'm good at my job, Jack.' She paused and bit her lip. 'At least, I was. And if it's something I can't sort easily, I'll leave it well alone and I'll help you find someone who can help. I'm not going to make things worse.'

'I didn't think for a moment that you would.'

'So you'll let me help?'

She didn't seem distressed; the thought of reverting to her old life, however briefly, hadn't reduced her to tears as the scones had done. She was confident in a way he'd never seen her before. And it got him wondering again exactly what had happened at her old company that had made her turn her back on something she obviously loved. Why hadn't she stayed and fought to keep her job?

None of his business.

'I was worried it might bring back memories you'd rather forget,' he told her. And she shook her head again.

'I want to help.'

There didn't seem any harm in letting her have a go. And goodness only knew he wasn't getting anywhere by himself. Claire hadn't been joking when she'd said there was a shortage of computer experts in the area.

He gave a short nod. 'If you're sure you don't mind . . . '

He didn't understand what she did, but she fixed the problem quickly and without fuss. Soon he and everyone else in the company were able to access their files and get on with their work.

'How can I thank you?' he asked.

'No need.'

'I think there is. Send me your bill and I'll make sure it's paid up straight away.'

She shook her head and he watched,

fascinated, as her ponytail swung backwards and forwards. And then she planted a hand on her hip and glared at him. She was magnificent when she was annoyed.

'What?' he demanded.

'I did this as a favour. To you and to Jessica. This isn't my job any longer. I don't expect to be paid for it.'

'Paula, be reasonable. You've helped me out of a very difficult situation here. If you hadn't turned up I'd have been stuck. I only want to compensate you for your time.'

'Really not necessary.'

'What about the café? Did you have to close it? You'll have lost money.'

'Your mother stepped in.'

There it was again — his mother being way too eager. He wished he could put his finger on why he was so uneasy about that.

But his mother wasn't the issue just now. A stubborn female had him in her sights and her dark eyes were flashing with something he didn't quite recognise.

She looked at him for a long moment. 'I'll tell you what — if you're so worried about it, you send me a bill for the times you've helped me. And I'll offset my charge and write you a cheque for the difference.' And with that she flounced out without a backward glance.

'You upset her,' Claire commented helpfully from the door.

'I know.'

'Did you mean to?'

He stared at the formidable sight of Claire with arms crossed and a dis-approving gleam in her eyes. 'Why on earth would I mean to upset Paula?'

Claire came into the office and sat down, uninvited. 'Oh, I don't know.' Claire cast him a withering glance. 'Maybe because she's an attractive, intelligent woman and she likes you? Maybe because you like her and you're scared witless.'

He felt his lips quirk, but stopped himself from laughing just in time. 'That doesn't make sense.'

She shrugged. 'I think you're scared of letting yourself be happy.'

'Claire.' He could easily lose patience, but his tone was still soft. 'I pay you to be my assistant, not my psychologist. And we both have a ton of work to catch up on after this morning.'

'I'm not moving until you understand what you've done.'

'OK.' He sat back in his black leather swivel chair and put his feet up on his desk. 'Why do you think I don't want to be happy?'

'I think you're worried about being disloyal to Sarah.'

He drew in a sharp breath at the mention of his late wife's name. People didn't mention Sarah around him much, and it was always a shock when they did. 'Don't be ridiculous.'

'I'm not being ridiculous. Why else would you shy away from another relationship?'

'Julie,' he reminded her. 'I went out with Julie for six months.'

'Julie doesn't count. She was never going to stay around in Kinbrae. And she would have been a rotten mother to

Jessica. She was way too selfish.'

He raised an eyebrow. 'You think?'

'I do. She wasn't interested in raising a family; she wanted to go off and do her own thing. And deep down you must have known that.'

'I don't have time for this.' He lifted his feet from the desk and planted them firmly on the ground, then he gestured towards the door. 'Close it behind you on the way out, please.'

'You're an attractive man, Jack.'

'And you're a married woman.'

She rolled her eyes. 'You're being deliberately obtuse. You know I don't see you that way.'

'But you think Paula does? Thinking like that is a bit outside the remit of an assistant.'

'If I don't say it, who will? You're an attractive man and Paula's lovely. And she likes you. And I think you like her.'

'She's not looking for a relationship either.'

'Did she say that?'

'Yes.'

Claire shook her head. 'She doesn't mean it.'

'She does.'

'Is that why she dropped everything and ran out here at a moment's notice?'

'Jessica asked her.'

'But she came over to help *you*.'

'We're friends, Claire. Nothing more. And there can never be anything more.'

Claire got to her feet, at last taking the hint that this conversation wasn't going anywhere. 'You're kidding yourself if that's what you truly think.'

'It can't be anything else.' Because Claire was right — he was scared. And he'd even chickened out of his plan to speak to his daughter last night.

'Whatever.' Claire was at the door now and she paused to look over her shoulder. 'In any case, you owe her an apology. Because you upset her, offering her money like that.' She closed the door with a bit more force than was necessary.

Jack found it very difficult to concentrate on his work — even though he now had peace and quiet and his computer was working.

★ ★ ★

'How was he?' Heather asked as Paula came back to the café.

'Jack? He was fine. We got the problem sorted and I told Claire to ring me if there's anything else she thinks I can help with.' She didn't add that she would have told Jack, but she was pretty sure he wouldn't have phoned her.

She didn't want to admit it, but she was very hurt that he hadn't called her when he was stuck and he would have known that she could have helped. There was no excuse for that. Not when she'd accepted his help on so many occasions.

Maybe he was like Adam. Maybe he didn't trust her to do a good job. Perhaps she'd told him too much about the circumstance of why she'd left London and taken over the café.

But Paula had always been honest

and open. That was who she was. And that was why she'd taken the blame when it had been handed out at her last company. Because, even though nobody had been able to explain exactly what had happened to the computer system that night, she had been on duty.

'What did you think of his offices?'

Paula sensed that Heather was eager to make conversation and she couldn't bring herself to be rude, so she smiled. 'Great,' she said. 'Very modern. When he told me where he worked I hadn't realised he was the JM of JM Structural Engineering.'

Heather laughed. 'I was so worried he was going to leave the area to find work,' she confided. 'He would have taken Jessica with him, too. But when he set up on his own it seemed like the best solution for everyone.'

'It would have been difficult for him without you,' Paula said. 'He's told me how much you've helped with Jessica over the years.'

Heather's smiled lit up her face. 'It's

been our pleasure. I know I probably shouldn't say it about my own grand-daughter, but she's such a sweetheart.'

Paula smiled. 'You've every right to say it, because it's true.'

'We're very proud of both of them, if I'm honest. Jack's done so brilliantly for himself — his company is doing phenomenally well. And it hasn't been easy for him, being a lone parent and a successful businessman.'

Yet again Paula found herself won-dering how Jack would take the news that McGregor's café had been sold to a stranger because of his parents' business worries. It was pretty obvious he would have been able to help out. And Paula guessed he'd be furious he hadn't been given the chance.

Still, it was nothing to do with her. And, even if she had felt guilty keeping the secret, Jack had made it perfectly clear today that he wanted to keep things between them on a purely professional footing.

She just about managed to stop

herself grinding her teeth at the thought.

* * *

It was late afternoon and Paula and Heather were tidying up as Jessica burst into the café, school bag slung over one shoulder.

'Thanks, Paula, for helping Dad today,' she said. 'I know he would have wanted to call you himself, but he's way too proud. He doesn't like to ask for help.'

'Just like his father,' Heather commented, and Jessica nodded.

'Yes, he and Granddad are exactly alike.'

'Right, young lady,' Paula said with a grin. 'The back room's empty, so why don't you go and do your homework. Then perhaps you can help out for half an hour if there's time.'

'Sure thing.' Jessica grinned as she made her way to the far door. 'I did most of my homework at Katie's after school. I'll be back in ten minutes.'

Paula smiled as she watched her go. Jessica reminded her so much of herself at that age: eager to take advantage of every opportunity — even if it meant hard work.

*   *   *

In the end, Jessica put in a good half-hour where she cleaned the kitchen and did a very good job. Heather promised to drop her home on her own way, and Paula had closed the blinds and was about to switch off the café lights, when she heard a gentle tapping at the door.

Startled, she went over and slid back the bolts. Opening the door a crack, she peered out to find a huge bunch of flowers, topped by a familiar shock of red hair on her doorstep.

# Visitors

She was tempted to quietly close the door in the face of those flowers. It was only her inbred good manners — coupled with her desire to find out what the man holding the flowers had to say for himself — that stopped her.

'Jack. You frightened the life out of me,' she told him as she opened the door wider and let him in.

'Sorry.' He grinned. And, despite the fact she was cross with him, and despite the fact she had no interest in him as a man, her heart flipped over in her chest. It was a very disconcerting experience. She took a deep breath and ignored it. And she also ignored the urge to smile back. 'What do you want, Jack?'

'I wanted to apologise.'

She turned and picked up a cloth and wiped the already spotless counter. 'What for?'

'For earlier. I upset you.'

She shrugged. 'Nothing to apologise for. I shouldn't have forced you to accept my help.'

He laughed softly and took the cloth from her and dropped it back on the counter. Then he dropped the bouquet of flowers into her arms and reached out and lifted her chin.

'Look at me,' he urged.

She sighed softly as she looked into his face. She couldn't be cross with him when he looked at her like that. 'It's fine,' she insisted. 'Honestly.' And she gave a little half-smile. 'And you didn't need to bring me flowers.'

'I can't think of anyone I'd rather give flowers to.'

She smiled then. She couldn't help it — the perfume from the roses alone would have ensured that, never mind the very handsome man who was smiling down into her eyes. She very gently placed the flowers onto the counter next to the cloth he'd taken from her.

'I'm sorry,' he said again.

Suddenly she felt all kinds of daft for having been so upset in the first place. All he'd done was what he'd thought was the right thing. After all, hadn't she done the exact same thing when she'd paid Heather for helping out at the café? And that gesture had been appreciated.

It wasn't Jack's fault that she'd thought the two of them were closer than that. That they could help each other out without obligation or expectation on either side. She wouldn't make that mistake in future.

But, when his hand moved around to the back of her head and he wound her ponytail around his fingers — she smiled for quite a different reason. He pulled her closer . . .

'Jack . . . I . . . ' She had no idea what she wanted to say, beyond his name.

'Whenever I see you,' he said, 'I'm overwhelmed by a need to kiss you. I wonder what that means?'

He sounded puzzled — as well he might. She was herself perplexed by the same thing. 'A kiss is just a kiss,' she told him. 'It doesn't have to mean anything . . . '

When his lips met hers, she realised she'd been deluding herself, and it did mean something. Something big. Adam's kisses had never been like this. They'd never left her breathless — or with her head reeling.

It was suddenly very obvious that the reason Jack affected her in the way he did was because she was thoroughly smitten by him. And she probably had been from the moment he'd walked through the door to the café on her first morning open.

*You're an idiot, Paula,* she told herself, even as she kissed him back. Falling for a man like Jack when she wasn't in the market for romance was just asking for trouble.

★   ★   ★

As her arms wound around his neck and her fingers entwined in his hair,

181

Jack gathered Paula closer.

'This is a bad idea,' she sighed against his mouth.

He had to agree. But she didn't make a move to stop kissing him and he wasn't inclined to put an end to it, either.

'Feels pretty good for a bad idea,' he couldn't help replying.

When he did eventually pull away, she clung to him for a moment, as though unsure she would be able to stand upright on her own.

'Have dinner with me tomorrow evening?' he asked. 'I'll get Mum to keep Jessica company for a couple of hours and we can head into town.'

She looked up at him with huge brown eyes and he held his breath. 'I'm sorry, Jack. I can't.'

He was crushed by her refusal and, in that instant, he realised what an idiot he was being. This wouldn't work for either of them. Why had he ever thought it would?

He'd eventually had a talk with Jessica in the car on the way back from her friend Katie's this afternoon. It had gone well. She'd been pleased that he and Paula were getting on. And she hadn't — unlike his mother — read too much into it. It had offered him hope. But, of course, that was useless unless Paula herself was on the same wavelength.

Which he realised now, with her refusal of his offer of dinner, that she wasn't.

He nodded. 'I understand. You've told me you're not interested — and I have Jessica to think about. It doesn't make sense to date when there's no future. I shouldn't have suggested it.'

'No,' she said. 'That's not what I meant.'

And, despite knowing in his head that it wasn't for the best, his heart began to hope. 'What did you mean?'

She pulled a chair from the nearest table and sank down onto it. 'I'm expecting visitors,' she said. 'My best friend and her husband.'

He grinned, suddenly thinking anything might be possible. She wasn't turning him down — it was just that someone else had prior claim on her time tomorrow.

'I was planning to make them dinner here,' she said. 'Nothing fancy, but if you feel up to taking the risk with my cooking, you'd be very welcome to join us.'

'You're sure?' He pulled up a chair for himself and sat down beside her. 'I wouldn't be intruding?'

'Of course you wouldn't. I'd like you to meet them. But I understand if you'd rather not.'

'Thank you, I'd like that.'

And it was true, despite the fact meeting a best friend was a big step and he really didn't think they were in that place yet.

'I'd better put those flowers in water,' she said, and he watched as she brought a vase full of water from the kitchen and began to arrange the stems. 'Gorgeous,' she said, a soft smile playing about her lips.

'I agree.' But he wasn't talking about the flowers.

She looked over and the look in her

eyes had him forgetting to breathe. 'I had another reason for coming over tonight,' he forced himself to say. 'Besides to deliver an apology.'

Her brown eyes narrowed. 'Oh?'

'Tell me exactly what happened. Why you left your job? Was the mistake really that terrible?'

The bloom in her hand shook and she looked away quickly. 'I've told you about it already,' she said.

'You told me there was some issue and you got the blame. You didn't tell me why you didn't stay and fight for a job you obviously love,' he reminded her. 'You said something about finding a new dream. But I'm not convinced that was true.'

She flushed a deep red and came back and sat beside him again. 'I thought of staying — riding out the storm.'

He resisted the urge to put his arm around her. 'Why didn't you?' he asked softly. 'Why did you run away?'

'Because sometimes it's easier to believe what everyone's telling you.

That it really is all your fault.'

'So, what if you could have a new dream, be your own boss doing what you've loved doing all your life, here in Kinbrae?'

She shook her head. 'I don't understand. There's nowhere around here with the kind of IT department I used to work in.'

'That's not what I meant. Why don't you start your own IT troubleshooting business? Do as you did today — help those in desperate need who aren't able to help themselves.'

She laughed. 'That would never work.'

'Why not? There was a guy who did exactly that, but he moved away. It's been very difficult to find someone reliable to replace him.'

'I find that very hard to believe. Thousands of teenagers could do what I did today. It wasn't that special.'

He shook his head. 'People won't want to trust their computers to thousands of teenagers. They want to deal with a professional. It wouldn't be quite what you're used to, but I saw earlier how much you loved problem-solving.'

'I don't know, Jack . . . '

He'd thought she might be reluctant. Whatever had happened had done a good job of denting her confidence. But now he'd planted the idea in her head, he hoped her subconscious might do the rest. He got to his feet. 'Just think about it. I know you're settling in here still, but there's no reason you couldn't run the café with Mum's help and set up a second business, too.'

She nodded. 'I'll give it some thought. But I don't know — it's taken time and a couple of McGregors on the books for people to trust me to serve them a cup of tea. Why would they let me near their computers?'

He paused for a moment then sighed. 'I'd employ you in a heartbeat.'

★   ★   ★

She did as she'd promised Jack she would and she gave the matter some thought. She thought about his words as the howling wind kept her awake that night. And she was still thinking when, at lunchtime the next day, Ellie and Andrew arrived at the café.

Joyce and Alice were in for lunch and Paula couldn't help smiling when she saw their very different reactions. 'What a fuss,' Joyce complained as Paula greeted her friends with hugs and laughter. 'I was hoping to enjoy a quiet lunch.'

Alice shook her head at her sister's reaction. 'They're only young. Leave them alone.'

Paula quickly introduced Ellie and Andrew to Joyce, Alice and Heather. 'My closest friends,' she added for good measure. And she couldn't believe how happy she was to see them.

'Why don't you take the rest of the day off,' Heather suggested. 'I've got everything covered here.'

Even though she'd taken a few hours out the day before, too, she was very tempted. 'It's not fair that I keep leaving you on your own,' she said, feeling she shouldn't go. 'I already left you on your own yesterday — I can't just swan off again.'

'Nonsense,' Heather said. 'I ran place for years. I can cope, you know.'

Paula laughed. 'Yes, I do know.'

'Besides, yesterday you were helping my son, so that doesn't count.'

Paula refused to acknowledge Ellie's interested expression. She guessed an inquisition would be imminent. Ellie would want to know about Heather's son . . .

★   ★   ★

'Heather's son . . . ?' Ellie started as soon as the door was closed to Paula's tiny flat.

Paula tried not to smile — and it wasn't only the thought of Jack that put her in a good mood. Her friend was nothing if not predictable.

'Nothing to tell,' she said, folding her arms as she made it clear she was not going to discuss the issue. 'You're both so tanned,' she marvelled in a blatant attempt to deflect her friend's interest.

'The weather in Hawaii was fab,' Ellie told her excitedly, and Paula gave silent thanks that her friend was so easily distracted. 'Such a gorgeous place. Though I don't suppose we'll ever get to go back.'

Paula smiled as Andrew gripped his new wife around the waist and danced around the cosy living room. 'We'll go back for our twentieth anniversary,' he promised.

And Paula couldn't help the soppy grin she knew had spread over her face. She was so pleased to see her friends this happy. And a tiny part of her wished she might one day have something similar.

Her smile dimmed and she frowned as a mental image of Jack instantly invaded her mind.

No.

Not going to happen.

'Have you left your bags in the car?' she asked. 'Why don't you fetch them and I'll put the kettle on.'

'They're at the hotel,' Ellie told her.

'You're staying in a hotel? But why? I've got room here . . . '

Ellie laughed. 'I know you mean well, but actually, no you haven't. You told me you've only got one bedroom.'

Paula shrugged. 'But I've always got room for you two. Seriously, I'll be fine on the sofa.' There was no hotel in Kinbrae, which meant they had to be staying in the nearby town of Aberbrig. It was only a short drive, but it would still mean she'd see less of them. Sleeping on the sofa was a small price to pay for time spent with good friends.

But her friends were having none of it and shouted her down. 'We're not throwing you out of your own bed,' Ellie insisted as Andrew shook his head to show he agreed. 'Now, we should make the most of this visit. I've never been to Scotland before. What is there to do around here?'

'If it was a nicer day I'd suggest going for a walk around the loch,' Paula said.

'But as it is, it might be an idea to drive into town where we can stay under cover as much as possible.'

'I'd like to go for a walk,' Ellie said. 'We've brought our waterproofs and I'd love to see a real Scottish loch. Besides, we've been in the car for a good few hours and it would be good to stretch our legs.'

'Are you sure? It's very windy out there,' Paula said as she glanced through the window at the looming dark clouds. 'And it looks as though it might rain again at any minute.'

If she was honest, she didn't mind the rain at all. And, even though she'd lived in Kinbrae for weeks, she was yet to see anything of the surrounding countryside. She hadn't really had time with being so busy with the café. And the rare hours she had taken off, she'd spent with Jack.

Hm. Jack again. He was creeping into her thoughts with alarming ease.

'It will be good to get some British rain after our honeymoon,' Ellie said with a laugh. 'I don't mean to rub it in about how lucky we were with the weather, but you can have too much of a good thing.'

'There is such a thing as too much sun,' Andrew agreed.

After living through the rains and the winds of Kinbrae for the past few weeks, Paula couldn't help but wonder if being in love had gone to their heads and affected their judgement. As far as she was concerned, there could never be too much sun.

★ ★ ★

They arrived back just as Heather McGregor was closing the café up for the night. 'Good time?' she asked as the thoroughly wet and windswept trio burst in through the door.

'It was bracing,' Paula told her with a smile, unable to think of anything more complimentary to say about their jaunt around the loch, then up to the top of Kinbrae Hill. They hadn't even been

193

able to see much of the view, either, with the weather being so murky.

'You're braver than me,' Heather said as she put her coat on and buttoned it up tight. 'I'm making straight for home, once I've collected Jessica. Denny's away on a job, so we're going to have a girly night in watching DVDs.'

'Thanks for that,' Paula said. 'Jack mentioned he'd ask if she could stay with you for a couple of hours while he's over here.'

'Oh, Jessica's never any bother. And it's nice that you've invited Jack to supper with your friends. All he's done for years is work and look after Jessica — it's time he got out to enjoy himself.'

'We're looking forward to meeting him,' Ellie said. 'Aren't we, Andrew?'

Andrew looked a little surprised. It was obvious he wasn't as quick on the uptake as his wife. 'Er . . . yes. Yes, we are.'

Paula locked up after Heather and braced herself. She knew what was coming. And she was proved right when

Ellie didn't even wait a minute before launching her questions. 'So,' she said, a huge grin on her face. 'Jack? Is he, by any chance, Heather's mysterious son?'

# Jessica

Paula winced as she saw the look of hope and interest on Ellie's face. They'd been friends for many years and there were some things you couldn't hide from someone that close. Not that she wasn't going to try.

'Yes,' she said, concentrating on keeping her tone neutral. 'He's a friend and he's helped me out a lot, so I thought it would be nice if he could meet my two best friends in the world. I think you'll all get on.'

'And Jessica?' Ellie asked.

'His daughter.'

'Oh, he's married?' Ellie made the assumption and Paula watched as her friend's face dropped. She couldn't allow that pretence to continue, though. If Ellie suspected she'd been misled, she would read an awful lot into the situation.

'Jack's a widower.'

She could see Ellie was about to ask more and decided to deflect her interest. It was one thing offering general information, but she didn't want to gossip about Jack's personal business — not even with her own best friend.

'I really enjoyed today,' she said. 'I'm so pleased you made the trip all the way up here because it's given me an excuse to take time off and see something of the area.'

She was adamant she needed to change the subject. The more she told her friend about Jack, the more unbearable the questioning would become. Ever since Ellie's engagement, she'd made it known she was keen to see her friend similarly settled. And Paula knew that whatever she said, Ellie was bound to suspect, on some level, that Jack might be a little more than a passing acquaintance.

But Ellie refused to be side-tracked. 'What's Jack like?' she asked.

'I hardly know him,' she said, meaning it. Really, if you looked at how little time they'd spent in each other's company, what she'd said was true. If you ignored the instant understanding they'd reached. And the kissing, of course. And she didn't examine too closely exactly why she'd chosen to invite someone who she claimed was just a friend to this quiet reunion between three people who'd known each other for years.

She knew Ellie would be wondering why he'd been included. And her friend would be wondering even more when she saw Jack. Because, however much Paula tried to put it to the back of her mind, there really was no ignoring the fact that he was utterly gorgeous.

★　★　★

The moment her friends met Jack that evening, Paula could see in their faces that their imaginations were working overtime. And she knew that protesting she thought of him as nothing more than a friend would be futile now. Ellie already had them marked as a couple; Paula could see it in her friend's expression and in the way she addressed questions to both of them.

Paula tried to keep the whole thing casual, but she could feel her face flush whenever she looked at Jack. And, despite herself, she couldn't stop the soft smile that turned her lips upward when he spoke to her. She knew her friends had noticed.

'You needed to meet someone else,' Ellie said as she followed Paula into the kitchen on the pretext of helping. 'You deserve someone nice. And Jack seems lovely, doesn't he?'

'He is.' She could have cut her tongue out with a rusty knife. Paula's reply had been based on pure instinct; her hopes of playing it cool had evaporated under the reality of spending even more time in his company and finding him nothing but lovely. But she really shouldn't have agreed so readily with her friend.

'Good. I'm glad you're admitting it. You were starting to embarrass yourself with your 'nothing more than friends' routine.' Ellie smiled to soften her words. 'I was worried that business with Adam might have put you off wanting to go out with anyone new.'

'We're not going out.'

'Not yet, maybe. But it can only be a matter of time. You seem very well suited.'

'I don't want to go out with anyone,' Paula said, keeping busy by taking their pudding from the oven so she didn't have to make eye contact with Ellie. 'And I've told him so.'

'You what? Well tell him you've changed your mind,' Ellie said.

'I can't.' Paula started to put the puddings onto plates and dust them with icing sugar. She could have taken the whole lot through and have everyone do that for themselves, but she'd quickly become accustomed to the café way of serving food.

'Why not?' Ellie demanded, and Paula could feel her friend's inquisitive gaze burning into her.

'Because it's not what either of us wants.'

'If you let him go you're a fool.' There was no nastiness about Ellie's words — she was offering advice, nothing more.

Paula stood back to admire her handiwork. She was really rather pleased with the individual bread and butter puddings — as she had been with the chicken pie that they'd eaten for their main course. She was very grateful for Heather's help in preparing the meal.

Eventually she dared to look up at Ellie. 'I can't let him go because I haven't got him,' she told Ellie — quite reasonably, she thought.

'I know why you're worried,' Ellie continued. 'But even I can tell he's nothing like Adam — and that's with only having met him an hour ago. How many times did you ask Adam to come to dinner with me and Andrew?'

'A few,' she mumbled. In the end she stopped asking because it was pretty obvious he hadn't been interested in her friends. And they had known that, too, which had made the few times they'd bumped into each other very awkward.

'And he never made it once. Whereas Jack's accepted the first time,' Ellie said. Though she didn't need to. Paula knew that Jack was nothing like the ex-fiancé who had let her down. For one thing, she couldn't imagine Adam being late to his own work so he could help her out by making scones. She giggled at the absurd picture that idea conjured up in her head.

'That's better,' Ellie said. 'Now let's get in there with the pudding before they come looking for us.'

They had started on coffee when Jack's mobile rang. 'I'm sorry,' he said, looking at the screen. 'I'd better take it; it's Mum.'

Paula watched with mounting horror as the blood drained from his face and wondered what could have provoked such a reaction.

'I'll be there as soon as I can,' Jack said. 'I'm sorry about this.' He got to his feet and found his jacket. 'It's Jessica. She's not well. Ryan's checked her over — my brother's a nurse,' he told Ellie and Andrew, by way of explanation. 'He doesn't think it's anything more serious than the virus that's doing the rounds, but she wants her own bed. So I'm afraid I have to go and get her.'

'Of course you must go.' Paula left the table and walked out to the car with him. 'Is there anything I can do?'

He smiled softly. 'No, it's fine. You go back to your friends, and please give them my apologies.'

'No apologies required. Everyone knows you have to go.' She stood on tiptoe and kissed his warm cheek and then sighed. 'Drive carefully. And let me know how she is when you can.'

\* \* \*

The party broke up shortly after Jack had gone. Ellie and Andrew were tired after the combination of the international flight and the long drive of the past few days. And everyone was worried about Jessica — even Ellie and Andrew, who were yet to meet her.

'We'll help tidy up before we go,' Andrew offered, but Paula shook her head.

'No need. You get off to your hotel, but come and see me before you leave, won't you?' she said, knowing that Heather would, in all probability, be too busy with her granddaughter to work at the café tomorrow. Jessica would be at home, she was sure — it was unlikely she would be well enough to go to school — and Jack wouldn't want to leave her on her own.

'Course we will,' Ellie said as she hugged Paula goodbye. 'Do you know,' she added, 'once things are back to normal at home, after the excitement of the wedding and the honeymoon, I'm really going to miss you living around the corner.'

'Me too,' Paula said.

She stood by herself, waving and wiping a tear from her eye as she watched their car drive around the corner. But oddly, even though seeing her friends reinforced how much she'd missed them, she couldn't think of going back now. This was her home and she didn't want to live anywhere else.

She cleared up, but the mundane task didn't take her mind from what Jack must be going through. Even though she knew Ryan was a good nurse and was to be trusted when he said it was only a virus, it was only natural that Jack would be worried about Jessica.

It was a little before midnight when the buzzing of her mobile interrupted her preparations for bed. She reached for the phone and her heart began to thump as the display showed the caller's name.

'Jack, how is she?'

She heard a heavy sigh down the phone. 'OK. She's suffered a bit since we got home, but she's sleeping now.'

'Is there anything I can do? Anything either of you need?'

'That's lovely of you, but we're both fine. I'm sorry about your dinner party.'

'Don't be silly — Jessica comes first. And there will be other chances for you to have dinner with Ellie and Andrew.'

There was a short silence at the other end and she knew she'd said too much. In an attempt to keep things light she'd suddenly given them a shared future. A future neither of them was supposed to want.

'Will there, Paula?'

She bit into her lip. And then made a decision. 'Yes,' she told him with certainty. 'Yes, there will.' Even if it was only as friends. But now she was honest enough to admit — if only to herself — that she hoped it might be as much more.

\* \* \*

Jack's jaw clenched as he ended the call. He tossed the phone to one side and raked a hand through his hair. It had been a rough few hours. Jessica was hardly ever unwell and, on the few occasions when she was, Jack found caring for her — worrying about her — extremely stressful.

Hearing Paula's voice, though, had been a comfort. He found himself wishing she was with him now. Having Paula by his side made most things better.

She was a good friend. The best friend he'd ever had. And if the fact he fancied her like crazy made him a little uneasy, it also made his heart soar.

★ ★ ★

Paula was on her own in the café the next morning when the Imrie sisters arrived, bearing a battered old laptop. 'You know all about computers.' Joyce made it sound like an accusation, and Paula had to make a concerted effort not to go on the defensive.

She managed a smile. 'I know a little bit.'

Alice put the laptop on the nearest table. 'I wonder if you could take a look at this, dear? It's been working terribly slowly and it always crashes before I can read my emails. I feel horribly out of touch.'

Paula raised an eyebrow. The sisters were really at extreme ends of the planet where technology was concerned. First you had Joyce, who regarded Paula's internet café ideas with nothing but hostility; then you had Alice, who was embracing the electronic age.

'Why don't you check your emails on one of my laptops here,' she invited. 'I'll bring over a pot of tea for you both and then I'll have a look at this.'

'Did you make those scones?' Joyce asked with a suspicious gleam in her eyes as she waved at a plateful of baking.

'No, they're all Heather's work.'

'In that case, we'll have a couple of the fruit ones to go with that tea.'

Alice winced, but Paula tried not to smile at the insult — she couldn't blame Joyce, not when Heather's baking was so good. And when her own was so bad.

There wasn't much wrong with the laptop that some TLC wasn't able to fix. Paula freed up some disc space by deleting some temporary files, then ran a couple of virus checks. Her heart nearly stopped when she saw the number of infections the machine had acquired. 'Alice, when did you last virus-check this laptop?'

Alice looked up, startled. 'Virus what, dear?'

Ah, OK. Paula took a deep breath. 'Do you buy anything online with your credit card? Or put in any passwords for online banking? Anything confidential?'

'No, I only use it for my emails. And to play games.'

She would never have had Alice down as a gamer, but she was relieved to hear that no confidential information had been punched in while the machine had been vulnerable.

'You know, I really can't believe you don't have a system for checking for viruses.'

Joyce shook her head in disapproval. 'You should have a firewall installed, too.'

'I thought you didn't know anything about computers,' Paula said in surprise.

'Of course I do,' Joyce snapped. 'Just because I don't want one rammed down my throat during my morning tea break, doesn't mean I don't appreciate how useful they can be.'

Paula frowned. Joyce was a secret surfer, it seemed. Which meant her objection to Paula's internet access in the café was more bluster than anything else. And it was at that point Paula realised her customer's grumpy demeanour really did have more to do with Joyce's own personality, rather than being anything to do with her disapproval of Paula.

# Jack's Discovery

All was well in Jack's world. His daughter had recovered from her recent illness and was back at school — and visiting a friend this evening. Business was going well. And he and Paula had agreed to take tentative steps to see where their relationship might lead. It was still early days, but he was hopeful things might work out. It had taken a while, but he'd reached a place where he was comfortable with the thought of a specific woman in his long-term future.

He decided to stop in at the farmhouse on his way home, to see if his mother might be free to collect Jessica from her friend's house later and keep her company for a couple of hours. He fancied taking Paula out and wanted to make sure his daughter would be taken care of before he suggested it.

'Hi,' he greeted as he walked into the

kitchen. Then he stopped dead as he saw his parents' expressions. Again he got the feeling there was something they weren't telling him. He grimaced and pulled a chair out for himself. 'What's going on?'

He noticed a look pass between his parents and he folded his arms as he waited for them to speak.

'Jack.' His mother got up from the table and hurriedly bundled some papers she and his father had been frowning over into a file. 'We weren't expecting to see you.'

'I gathered.'

He saw his mother glance across at his father. 'We've got to tell him, Denny.'

His father grimaced and then shrugged. 'Go on, then.'

Jack listened as they talked. It wasn't pleasant news, but it could have been worse. Lack of money could cause worry and could make you miserable, but it was never the end of the world. And it was something he could help with. He was, however, not best pleased to have been left out of this particular loop.

'You should have told me,' he said quietly.

'So you could do what?' his father asked gruffly. 'Offer to help out?'

'Yes.'

'We couldn't let you do that,' his mother said. 'You have Jessica to think about. And you never know what's going to happen in the future with your own company.'

'My company's sound. And I have enough put by to cover any emergencies. Including helping my parents out.'

'No,' his father said. 'We couldn't take money from you.'

'I don't understand. Why not? You provided me and Mark and Ryan with the best of everything as we were growing up. Don't you think we deserve the chance to help you out when you need it?'

His father refused to meet his eye and instead took a huge interest in the fingers Jack drummed against the scrubbed wood of the kitchen table.

'I know you're angry,' his mother said

as she walked over to his side of the table and put a hand on his shoulder. 'But give it a few years and maybe you'll understand.'

'How will I ever understand that you kept something like this from me?' He frowned.

His father shook his head. 'When Jessica grows up and has made her own fortune,' he said, 'come back and tell me that you'd be happy to take money from her.'

'I'll make us all a cup of tea,' his mother said as she moved over to put the kettle on. 'Then we can talk sensibly and gain some perspective on this.'

'Not for me, thanks, Ma. I'd better get going.' He would forgive his parents, he knew he would. But he was hurt they hadn't trusted him.

He needed to get out of there as soon as he could.

He needed to see Paula.

★  ★  ★

Things were quiet in the café. Paula would have closed up early, but she was always hopeful a customer might pop in at the last minute, so she hung around.

When the tinkling bell warned of an arrival a few minutes later, she abandoned her cleaning of the kitchen surfaces and flew through to the café. Her smile was instantaneous.

'Hi, Jack.' And then she noticed his expression. 'What's wrong?'

His breath was expelled in one loud hiss and he covered the distance between them in a few short strides. 'Hi,' he said, before he gathered her closed and buried his face in her hair.

Even though she knew there had to be something very wrong, she sighed with contentment as she was enveloped in the heat from his body, and her arms reached around his waist to hug him back. 'Is it Jessica?' She'd hardly dared to ask the question — that something might be wrong with Jessica was unthinkable. But something had upset him.

'Jessica's fine,' he said. 'She's at a friend's house.'

She sighed with relief, even though he was holding her so tightly she could barely breathe. They stood for long minutes with their arms around each other and her heart ached for him. She knew he was upset and she was reluctant to ask any other questions until he was ready to talk. Knowing Jessica was OK, though, took some of the pressure off for now.

'I know it's early,' he said, letting her go at last. 'But can you close up? I need to get away from everyone for a while.'

She nodded and he helped her close the blinds. She stopped only to grab her jacket and then they were out of the door.

'Where do you want to go?' she asked as they headed for his car.

'Somewhere I can breathe.'

He drove them out towards the loch and they walked to the shore in silence.

'Do you want to tell me what's wrong?' she asked at last. It seemed he wasn't going to offer the information without a prompt. And her head was dizzy with all the thoughts of what it might be. Even while she was unbearably glad that she was the one he'd run to when he needed someone.

'I hate it when people keep secrets from me.'

Paula's heart was heavy with guilt. Though if he'd found out that she'd been keeping the news about his father's business from him, she was pretty sure his greeting would not have been as enthusiastic.

He picked up a pebble and threw it into the loch and, even though the light was fading, they were able to see the ripples spread out across the clear water.

'I can handle just about everything else.' He sighed heavily. 'But I really can't cope with being kept in the dark — particularly when there's something I could do to help.'

She reached out and put her hand on his arm. 'What's happened, Jack?'

There was a brief silence and his jaw clenched as he stared out towards the waters of the loch. 'I found out why Mum sold the café.'

'Oh.' Her hand dropped to her side and she only just resisted the urge to shudder with horror. She'd known keeping the information from him had been a bad idea, but what could she have done? It hadn't been her secret to share. 'Who told you?'

He swung around to look at her, his blue eyes clouded with confusion. And then, after a moment, he slowly nodded. 'You knew.'

It wasn't a question, but she nodded anyway. 'I'm so sorry, Jack. Heather asked me not to say anything.'

*　　*　　*

This news floored Jack. Possibly more so than his parents' earlier revelations. Even though he hadn't known her long, he'd trusted her. More than he'd ever trusted anyone. It had been instinctive.

And now he felt so let down. He watched as she bit her lip and looked up at him with anxious brown eyes. And, even while he disliked intensely that she'd kept the news from him, he still wanted to gather her up and hold her close.

'How did you find out?' he asked her.

'Your mum needed work and she told me why. I don't think she meant to tell me. I think it was just that she needed to offload to someone who wasn't involved.'

He didn't reply.

She took a deep breath. 'Your parents kept quiet for the best of reasons, Jack. They didn't want to burden you and your brothers with something like that when you have your own lives to lead. You mustn't be angry with them.'

He wasn't angry — not really. More shocked, as he really hadn't been expecting anything like this. And he definitely hadn't expected Paula would keep secrets from him.

Jack needed to tell her how he felt. He wanted to share with her his disappointment at being kept in the dark. Most of all, he wanted to tell her how much she had come to mean to him and how much it hurt that she could keep a secret of this magnitude from him. Particularly when she must have known he would want to know.

He raked a rough hand through his hair. He didn't know where to begin, so he turned away. It hurt too much to look at her lovely face — and its silent pleas for understanding. It was much easier to do what he'd done for many, many years if something had bothered him: he brooded alone.

That had been his major problem, he could see that now. The past wee while he'd begun to believe that he'd found his soul mate in Paula. He'd hoped she was someone with whom he could share his fears and his dreams and his deepest thoughts. He was shattered to find the feeling was not reciprocated.

'Jack?' Her hand was on his arm again. He craved that contact and stepping away from her hurt. But he had to do it.

And he schooled his features so that none of his bitterness or disappointment showed when he turned back to face her.

'It's probably time I took you home,' he said. Despite his best efforts, his voice was flat. Even he could hear it.

'I thought you needed to breathe?'

'I've had all the air I can handle for one night.' His laugh was without humour. 'Besides, I need to collect Jessica.' That was true — despite the fact that had been his reason for visiting the farmhouse tonight, his parents' revelation had pushed that thought out of his mind.

'OK,' she said as she began to walk back to the car. 'Let's go back.'

His heart recognised he was making a mistake in pushing her away, but his head knew it was the only way.

# A Nasty Surprise

It had been a busy day in the café — following on from a night of hardly any sleep. Paula was looking forward to the time when she'd be able to say goodnight to her customers, wave good-bye to Jessica, who was due in at any minute, and close up. A long, hot bath, she thought, might restore her sprits a little. And then she planned to have an early night.

Paula knew exactly why she'd been unable to rest properly last night: she'd known she'd let Jack down, and she hated herself for that. OK, she knew there had been no way she could have betrayed Heather's confidence. But, once she'd found out what had been going on with the haulage firm, she should have convinced Heather to tell her sons.

He hadn't said a word last night to make her think he blamed her, but she knew she owed Jack a huge apology. And, as soon as she saw him, that would be the first thing she would do.

In the meantime, she'd tried to put Jack from her mind — but proved to be spectacularly unsuccessful with the task. No matter what she did, no matter how bright a smile she put on for her customers, nor how busy she kept herself, he would keep popping into her mind and catching her unawares.

'Jessica, can you clear that corner table, please?' she asked as the teenager, having stored her bag and coat away, reported for duty.

'Sure,' she replied, and she went off with a smile.

Paula smiled too, as she thanked her good luck that Jessica was fitting in so well to life at the café. Grabbing a cloth, Paula started to wipe a table down, when the tinkling of the bell urged her to turn to see who had arrived.

She peered through narrowed eyes at the man. She was sure she recognised him, but she couldn't quite place his face . . .

Then she realised who he was. 'Hello Adam.' She couldn't bring herself to smile. In an odd way, he looked almost like a stranger — someone she'd known in another lifetime. She found it hard to believe she'd ever planned to marry him and share her life with him. She could think of nothing worse now.

'Great to see you, Paula.' He leaned over and kissed her cheek. His lips were cold and she struggled not to wince. It was one thing being friendly to an ex-fiancé; quite another being friendly to an ex-fiancé who had encouraged you to leave the job you loved and had then ended your relationship without warning or explanation.

'I've missed you,' he added.

'Oh.' She knew the polite thing to say would have been that she'd missed him, too, but she hadn't and she couldn't bring herself to lie about it.

His mouth tightened as he noticed her lack of response. 'Is there somewhere quiet where we can talk?'

'Yes, of course.' She waved him to the corner table that Jessica had just cleared. 'This will be quiet enough. Please, sit.'

'I had hoped there might be somewhere a bit more private.'

She glanced around at the couple of occupied tables and then at Jessica, who was behind the counter. She met the teenager's worried glance and smiled reassuringly, before assuming a pleasantly inert expression as she turned her attention back to Adam.

They could have talked in the smaller side room — it was empty of customers at the moment — but she didn't want to encourage him. Besides, he'd lost any right to demand to speak to her in private.

'I'm afraid I can't leave the café just now,' she told him. 'But we'll be fine to talk here.'

He didn't look convinced, and he was probably right to have reservations as everyone left in the place, including

Jessica, watched them with way too much interest. But he did as he was told and sat down.

'Can I get you a drink or something to eat?'

He shook his head. 'No, nothing, thank you. I'm here to talk to you.'

She looked at him and wondered how she could have ever thought him handsome. He wasn't as tall as Jack, his jaw not nearly as strong, and his face nowhere near as attractive. And Adam's receding blond thatch was decidedly dull in comparison to Jack's full head of red hair.

She hoped her smile was chilly — that was certainly the effect she was striving for. 'Is there anything left to say?'

There was an earnest light in his eyes as he leaned forward and took hold of her hand. 'Paula, I made a mistake.'

She snatched her hand back from his cold grip. She had no desire for him to touch her and she didn't want to leave him in any doubt of the fact. 'A mistake? I'm sorry, I don't quite understand.'

His face was flushed from the

hand-holding slight and his smile was rather forced as he sat back in his chair. 'Letting you go was the worst thing I've ever done.'

Realisation dawned. He'd come to ask her to take him back.

She stared at him, wondering what she should say. She didn't want to be cruel, but there was no point in giving him false hope. Looking back, she knew she'd been miffed at the time — but her lack of upset at the break-up had shown her quite clearly that they really weren't meant to be together. She hadn't even cried. In fact, she'd been a lot more emotional about losing her job.

'I want you to come back with me,' he said, when she didn't speak.

Her jaw dropped and she could still find no words. She was vaguely aware of Jessica leaving a tray of tea they hadn't ordered on the table, but she was too shocked to acknowledge her.

She'd barely thought of him at all since she'd arrived here in Kinbrae, unless it had been in relation to what had happened at work.

What should she say to him now? She couldn't think. She knew she definitely didn't want to go back — neither with him nor to him. She was happy here now. She was happy in Kinbrae, fending off Joyce's grumpy complaints, joking with Heather and Jessica as they worked. And she was happy with Jack. Even if Jack wasn't too happy with her at the moment.

'Adam . . . I . . . '

'I shouldn't have let my personal issues cloud my judgement where work was concerned. I was so worried people might think I was favouring you that I forgot you were the best person for the job. I should have convinced you to stay.'

Relief overwhelmed her. He was talking about work. Well, she still had no intention of returning, but at least things would be less messy if it wasn't personal.

'Why would they think you were favouring me?'

'Well, you know . . . that business with the system crashing. If I was seen to support you . . . '

She shook her head. 'You know, Adam, the more I go over it in my head, the more I'm certain I did nothing wrong.' She'd thought about it since talking the matter over with Jack. And Jack's confidence in her abilities had convinced her. She'd been used as a scapegoat.

As she watched, Adam paled. 'Well, I had to blame someone.' He clamped his mouth tightly shut, but the words were already out.

'It was you,' she said as realisation dawned. 'You made the mistake and passed it off as mine.'

His pallor became suffused with red — and then purple. She seriously suspected he might be about to blow a major artery. 'Well, what could I do?' he blustered. 'I would have lost my job.'

'So you fixed it so they'd blame me?'

'The bosses were more lenient with you than they would have been with me. They didn't sack you — but as the departmental manager, I'd have been expected to resign.'

She sighed heavily. '*I* felt I was expected to resign. Didn't you feel you should have said something then?'

'We were getting married.' He shrugged. 'You'd have given up work once we'd had children in any case.'

She shook her head. Had she ever really known this man at all? Had he ever really known her? 'No, I wouldn't have. I loved my work — I'd studied hard to get my qualifications. I wouldn't have given it all up if we'd had children.'

She was aware of a presence at the table and looked up to find Joyce Imrie wearing her customary frown. 'Is anyone serving? Or should I go behind the counter and make my own cup of tea?'

'I'm sorry, Joyce.' She looked around for Jessica, but she was nowhere to be seen. 'Jessica must have slipped out.' She got to her feet and began to walk towards the kitchen. 'Tea, was it?'

She was so furious it wasn't true. She

couldn't believe she'd allowed a lowlife like that to make her doubt herself. And she couldn't believe he had the cheek to turn up now to attempt to get her to go back to the job she'd left because of him.

'Who's that?' Joyce had followed her over and was nodding towards the corner they'd just left.

'Nobody important,' Paula said, trying not to grind her teeth. 'Why don't you take a seat and I'll bring your tea over.'

She refused to look at him — didn't trust herself to keep her cool if she did. But she could feel his eyes on her — and she could feel he was displeased with the reception he'd received. She nearly laughed at that thought as she prepared a tray for Joyce with teapot, cup, saucer, milk jug, sugar . . .

By the time she went back to the corner of the café where Adam sat, she was ready to ask some questions. 'So why did you end our relationship if you knew you'd blamed me unfairly for what happened?'

He sighed. 'Please don't be angry with me. Management were putting pressure on me — once you'd left the company they weren't happy we were still seeing each other.'

'That's ridiculous. Why would they care?'

He shrugged. 'Because you left so suddenly, there was a query over industrial sabotage.'

Paula sank back into her chair. 'And, rather than stick up for me — rather than tell everyone it had been your mistake — you let them all think me capable of that.'

He shrugged again. 'I thought, once the dust had settled, we could take up where we'd left off.'

She laughed. So he was hoping for a reconciliation. 'You think I'd take you back after that?'

How could she have misjudged Adam's character so badly? The man had no backbone at all. Really not the kind of man any girl should hope to rely on.

'I'd thought you were joking when

you'd said you were buying a café.' He looked around and wrinkled his nose. 'I was shocked when your mother told me you'd settled in this place — and that you were living above the shop.'

That was the final insult for Paula. 'This is what I want,' she told him, knowing at last exactly what she needed to do. What she should have done as soon as he'd walked through the door. She looked at him calmly and levelly, so he'd know she wasn't in the least emotional. Well, not beyond the emotion of being furious with him for ruining her career.

'I think you'd better leave, Adam. We don't have anything to say to each other.'

'Don't be silly. Run along and pack a bag and we can get out of this place and back to civilisation. We can put this café on the market and get married, just like we planned. I've convinced the bosses you're not a threat to their company; they'll be happy enough to see us settled now.'

She was aware of Joyce and a couple of other customers taking a huge interest in the conversation, but she didn't care. This was her home now, and she had no intention of allowing Adam or anyone else to browbeat her into leaving.

'You're not hearing me. I said no. I'm not interested in going back with you, and there's no way on earth you could persuade me to marry you.'

His face registered surprise and Paula tried not to laugh — and failed.

'You'll regret this.'

She shook her head, still laughing. 'I don't think so. Thank you for dropping by, but I think it's best if you don't call again.'

The chair scraped against the floor as he got to his feet. 'You will fail here. And you will come crawling back to me,' he promised, his face every bit as purple as before. 'But don't leave it too long — I'm not going to hang around indefinitely.'

Relief made her knees weak as she

watched him go. She couldn't believe she hadn't realised he had been behind the mistake that had cost her a career. But why would she have? True, he'd ended their relationship to save his own job, but he why would she have suspected a man who was supposed to be in love with her of framing her?

One thing she was sure of now, though — even if things were never to work out between herself and Jack, she never wanted to see Adam again as long as she lived.

# A Decision

Everything happened for a reason. Jack had discovered the hard way over the years that the saying was true. And if the haulage business hadn't been in trouble and his mother hadn't felt a need to sell the café, then Paula wouldn't have been brought into their lives. So, in a roundabout way, it had been a good thing his parents hadn't told him they needed help.

He was in his home office, unable to concentrate on the piles of work he'd brought back with him. He'd wanted to be here when his daughter arrived home from her shift at the café. But now he was thinking he should maybe head over to speak to Paula once she'd closed up.

He'd been shocked yesterday when he'd found out he hadn't been told about his parents' money worries. But now he'd calmed down and had time to think, he could understand it. His father had been right — there was no way he'd ever expect or want Jessica to help him out financially in the future. So it was entirely reasonable his parents would feel the same way about accepting help from him and his brothers.

As for Paula, well, there was nothing really to blame her for. She'd kept his mother's confidence, even though it must have been very difficult for her to do so. He was ashamed now of his reaction last night — towards his parents and towards Paula. And, even though he hadn't said much to either party, he had thought plenty.

He was so accustomed, though, to sorting out everyone's problems. It had been a shock to discover nobody had asked him to help this time.

For the second time since he'd met her, he realised he owed Paula a huge apology.

The front door crashed open. 'Dad,' Jessica called, and he heard her footsteps run up the hall. She was early. He hadn't expected to see her for at least another half-hour.

'I'm in the study,' he called back, and a moment later she threw the door open.

'Dad, you need to come quick.' Her face was flushed and she was out of breath.

He was immediately on his feet. 'What is it? Are you hurt?'

'It's Paula,' she gasped, as she tried to get her breath back.

'Paula's hurt?'

'No — but there's a man at the café and I heard them talking. He wants Paula to leave and go back to the city with him. Dad, you've got to stop her.'

When Julie had told him she was leaving for the city, he'd accepted her decision without question. It hadn't even occurred to him to try to dissuade her. But life without Paula was unthinkable. And he knew he had to try to talk her out of going.

'Hurry, Dad,' Jessica pleaded as he continued to stand there.

Paula swept the floor and adjusted the blinds across the windows and the door. It had been a funny few days and she was keen to go up to her flat to relax in that bubble bath she'd been looking forward to before her shock visitor had arrived.

Now she knew the computer troubles at her old place of work had definitely been nothing to do with her, she was ready to think about Jack's suggestion of setting up an IT trouble-shooting venture. With Heather and Jessica helping here, she knew she'd be able to run both businesses alongside each other. She was excited to think she might work with her beloved computers again. And, even if the type of work she was thinking of now wasn't exactly what she'd trained for, it was close enough.

She glanced around one last time and was about to head upstairs when she was startled by a sharp knock on the glass of the door. The blinds were closed; it would be obvious to everyone that the café was shut.

She shook her head. She was in no mood for further visits. But if it was Adam, she would be ready for him this time and she'd tell him exactly how she felt about him. She threw back the locks and swung open the door.

Her heart missed a beat. 'Jack!' she exclaimed with genuine pleasure. Then she remembered how upset he'd been last night, and she held her breath as she tried to gauge his mood. His smile was hesitant and gave little away. 'Jack,' she said again, softer this time. 'I'm sorry I didn't tell you about the haulage business . . . ' she started, but he held up his hand.

'It's me who owes you an apology. Can I come in?' He kicked the door closed behind him and, before she could say another word, she was in his arms and his lips crashed down on hers as though his life depended on it.

She was breathless and light-headed when he eventually allowed her up for air, and she was grateful when he dragged out a chair and pulled her onto his lap. She reached out and traced his strong jaw with her fingers and he lifted her hand to his mouth and pressed his lips against her palm.

'Don't go,' he said. 'Please. I know I've been a bit slow on the uptake, but when Jessica told me you were planning to run away to the city with some strange man, I realised how much you mean to both of us. We both adore you. In fact, I'm quite madly in love with you and I don't know what I'd do without you.'

She wound her arms about his neck, pure joy filling her heart as she smiled into his eyes. 'I love you, too. And if Jessica hadn't abandoned her shift halfway through, she'd have heard me refuse Adam's offer.' She smiled. 'Not only did he admit he'd framed me for a mistake he'd made himself, but I realised as soon as I saw him that I'd never been in love with him.'

He grinned. 'But you are in love with *me*?'

She nodded. 'I just said so.' She just couldn't stop grinning. To have Jack confirm he felt the same way about her as she did about him was beyond anything she could have expected.

'Then will you stay in Kinbrae forever?'

She nodded again.

'And will you marry me?'

She pretended to think for a moment. 'Joyce Imrie would be pleased if I said yes.'

He shook his head. 'What's Joyce Imrie got to do with anything?'

'It offended her terribly that a non-McGregor was running the café. If I marry you, it would correct that anomaly.'

'In that case, how can you refuse me?'

'I can't,' she said as she kissed him again.

## THE END